YO-AGA-495

THE FORTEC CONSPIRACY

by Richard M. Garvin
and Edmond G. Addeo

A SIGNET BOOK
Published by The New American Library

Library of Congress Catalog Card Number: 68-13286

The authors gratefully acknowledge permission from G. P. Putnam's Sons and John Fuller for permission to quote from *Incident at Exeter,* copyright © 1966 by John Fuller.

This is a work of fiction. All persons, places, institutions, and events portrayed are not to be construed as real.

This is an authorized reprint of a hardcover edition published by Sherbourne Press, Inc.

SIGNET TRADEMARK REG. U.S. PAT. OFF. AND FOREIGN COUNTRIES
REGISTERED TRADEMARK—MARCA REGISTRADA
HECHO EN CHICAGO, U.S.A.

SIGNET BOOKS are published by
The New American Library, Inc.,
1301 Avenue of the Americas, New York, New York 10019

FIRST PRINTING, APRIL, 1969

PRINTED IN THE UNITED STATES OF AMERICA

FAMILY REUNION

Barney Russom slowly swung open the door to the inner sanctum. His heart seemed to catch like cloth on a nail as he took in the room before him, the tables, the microscopes, the complex equipment.

He hardly noticed them. He went half-eagerly, half-fearfully, to the transparent tube hanging on the wall. He gazed into it. And froze.

There, facing outward like a deformed piece of statuary, was the shriveled ochre prune that had once been his brother, Captain Robert Russom, who had seen what no man could afford to see and live.

And now it was Barney's turn . . .

Recent SIGNET Science Fiction

to
John M. Garvin
and
Edmond G. Addeo, Sr.

Like one that on a lonesome road
Doth walk in fear and dread,
And having once turn'd round, walks on,
And turns no more his head,
Because he knows a frightful fiend
Doth close behind him tread.

Samuel Taylor Coleridge
Rime of the Ancient Mariner

THE FORTEC
CONSPIRACY

CHAPTER 1

The room, of course, was filled. When Dr. Bernard M. Russom gave a press conference, every trade journal reporter on the West Coast tried to attend.

Fifty shadowed faces and a hundred shadowed eyes moved with Barney as he took the rostrum.

"The United States can eavesdrop on more than one intelligent civilization elsewhere in the universe any time we're ready to set up the gear."

Pencils moved quickly, murmurs grew.

"All we need," Barney went on, "is the money. Not the hardware, not the equipment, not the know-how. All we need is the dough." A few of the reporters chuckled at Barney's eschewing of the normal couching of terms in technical jargon. "There are thousands —thousands—of interstellar worlds that are capable of having civilizations with communication equipment. With our current technology, we can listen in on them and perhaps be the first ones outside their own planet to do so. And this, gentlemen, would be the most significant development of mankind in his entire history on Earth."

A hundred eyes grew intense, pencils scratched.

"We can and we must do it," Barney went on. "How?" He turned to the blackboard behind him and stroked a stark white line across its length. "A receiving antenna such as we have developed in the past few years can be constructed . . ."

Hours later, at the end of a long and tiresome day, Barney Russom was finally alone.

It was February, and in adherence to the peculiar reversal of seasons in California, the Palo Alto hills

11

behind Stanford University were somewhere between the lush viridity of winter and the barren brown of spring.

From his walnut-paneled office, Barney could see the Stanford Cross, a series of giant parabolic antennas that comprised the sophisticated radio telescope of the University. He had looked at this scene thousands of times—the impersonal and seemingly formidable intrusion of advanced scientific technology onto nature's private and passive repose.

Drowsy clusters of memories churned within him. He thought of the rugged seacoast on the other side of the hills and the rocky beaches that had provided him and his twin brother so many peaceful moments when they were studying together at Stanford.

How far he had come. How remote those days were now. Barney stood casually as he gazed out the window. At thirty-eight he retained the hard but supple physique of his college days. Light wisps of grey were beginning to sprout at his temples; his skin was clear and tanned. His eyes were alive and intense—almost translucent blue. Barney lit a cigarette, squinting as the first curls of smoke reached his eyes.

He found himself thinking of his brother Bob. For some inexplicably sudden reason he wondered what his brother was doing. Was he, too, enjoying the mental tour of youthful days, careless weeks during Easter vacation, fishing at Santa Cruz? Thoughts of Bob flashed randomly through his mind—how exactly they were alike, physically and mentally—how they acted the same, thought the same, how often words were not even needed.

How Barney would be about to suggest a beer after their last class when Bob would poke him, saying, "Christ, I'm thirsty." How both were quick to anger, and both would fall into quiet solitude at the sight of a dead animal lying by the road. How, only three weeks ago, Barney had placed a call to his brother in Ohio, only to get a busy signal in reply because Bob was calling him. And Barney thought, too, of the subtle differences between them—the argument they had had when they were choosing careers. Bob chose medicine and the Air Force, Barney chose physics and industry. Barney wasted no time in marrying after graduation, and Bob had married just three years ago. Barney had no children, though, and Bob now had a one-year-old daughter.

Barney had been trying for a year to talk Bob into taking a teaching position at Stanford, because he wanted Bob closer. He deeply missed his brother.

Barney snapped back to the present. Now he was Vice-President and Director of Research for Pace International. A graduate *summa cum laude* in electronics engineering and physics, he had originated P-I along with Marshall Pace, a classmate. The company was now thirteen years old, with an annual sales volume of more than one hundred million dollars. It was Barney's engineering skill, more than anything else, that had catapulted Pace International into *Fortune* magazine's "Top Five Hundred." He was proud that the instruments he designed were being used all over the free world, from a small hospital in Cambodia to an airborne package pulsing somewhere in the sky.

Time was Barney's nemesis. If he was sometimes a stranger to his family, he was a blood brother to the burgeoning electronics fraternity. As a member of this brotherhood, he was continually hounded by people with problems. If Monty Kuehner over in Research, or the Governor of the state, couldn't reach Barney, it was a good bet he was in Washington lunching with the Secretary of Defense.

He had given a press conference that morning, and the idea he advanced was causing the scientific community to turn its head once again in the direction of Barney Russom. The impact was varied, ranging from mild sniggers to outrageous telephone calls. His theory had previously been presented at a local meeting of the I-Triple-E (an acronym for the Institute of Electronics and Electrical Engineers), but the press conference had been hastily called to appease the local reporters.

He had long contended there were thousands of highly developed civilizations in the universe, and today he explained in detail how a six-mile-wide radio telescope, consisting of hundreds of receivers, could be constructed in the Nevada desert. With this enormous ear, man could hear signals produced by other intelligent societies.

Now he had to grant one last interview for today. Norman Fine, another faceless trade journal editor, was in the lobby. Although the aftermath of the press conference and the cacophony of jangling telephones had made him irritable, he walked out and spoke courteously to Fine. Then, the day behind him, he decided to go home and work on his seminar address for next month's national I-Triple-E convention in New York City.

He knew the subject of that speech would start it all over again.

Barney steered the dark green Morgan into the driveway of his early-California home in the Palo Alto hills. His wife was at a little theater rehearsal, so he pressed a small red button under the dashboard of the vintage automobile he had restored himself. The lights of the house silently lit themselves and the front door swung open. Turpin, his cross-eyed German shepherd, bounded out the door and greeted him with a yelp.

"You know, Turp," he called to the dog, "someday I'm going to patent that gadget and we're both going off to the Riviera."

Barney picked up the evening paper and strode into the house. The door closed behind him, automatically locking itself. "Well, I know you had a better day than I did, Turp, so you'll just have to wait until I fix myself a drink. Then you'll get your dinner."

Barney went directly to the sideboard in the living room and removed a bottle of Scotch.

He made a drink and took the bottle into the kitchen. The feeding ritual was about to take place. He always enjoyed watching Turp's tail wag faster and faster as he called off the various types of canned dog food. But tonight at the first mention of food, the dog whined and retreated to a corner.

Surprised at so obvious a break in their sacred tradition, Barney put the bottle down and walked over to Turpin. He knelt next to him.

"What's the matter, Turp? Aren't you hungry?"

The dog didn't move. He eyed Barney dolefully.

"You're not getting sick on me, are you?" Barney said. He felt the dog's nose and stood up. "I'll tell you what. How about a raw egg in your chow as an extra treat? I'll leave it here for you."

After preparing the dog's dinner, Barney picked up the bottle again and went into his study to go over the draft of his convention address.

At eight-thirty that evening, while he was still alone in his study and halfway through his speech, the telephone rang. It was Ginger, his sister-in-law in Ohio. She was hysterical.

Barney was momentarily frightened when he heard her incoherent sobs. Ginger's voice came over in broken sentences.

"Barney," she muttered distractedly. "Barney, it's Bob. His commander was just here."

Barney felt a rising panic. "What's the matter, Ging? Is he hurt?"

She didn't reply immediately, and Barney heard her trying unsuccessfully to control her weeping. "Ginger!"

"Barney, he . . . he . . ." She paused, breathing heavily. "He's dead, Barney! They said he killed himself." She continued to scream the ugly news and her words punched harshly into the pit of Barney's stomach.

"No," he said to himself, dazed.

Captain Robert W. Russom of the United States Air Force had been an outstanding histopathologist stationed at Wright-Patterson Air Force Base. Now, he no longer existed.

CHAPTER 2

One of the largest Air Force bases in the United States sprawls officiously just northeast of Dayton, Ohio. Wright-Patterson is a vast complex of thousands of multi-purpose buildings and laboratories. The bleak conglomeration of quonset huts, hangars, sheds, and administration buildings assaults one with functionality.

Most of the more than twenty-seven thousand personnel at Wright-Patterson work on projects that fall outside routine military activities. For this reason, many areas of the base are restricted, protected by both armed guards and unseen but all-seeing eyes of electronic security systems. Planes come and go with startling frequency, almost five hundred daily. Large, ponderous cargo carriers, jet fighters, and bombers foul the air with kerosene fumes. Official cars bully their way across the base. Privates, generals, and government dignitaries hurry grim-faced through doorways and gates.

The noise of monstrous wind tunnels competes for attention with warning alarums. The clamor and boom of rolling fuel drums and jet engines comprise the background theme for the most sense-battering vision of all: the steady arrival of the Vietnam dead in their olive-drab cans.

The only quiet moment is at dusk, when all pause in fleeting respect as the flags are lowered and a tinny *Retreat* crackles from rusty loudspeakers.

One division of the base is different from the rest in both physical arrangement and mission. Down black-topped Hebble Creek Road, in the southeast corner of the base, is FORTEC—The Foreign Technology Division of the Air Force. The mission of FORTEC is to study and evaluate the technical capabilities of all real and potential enemies of the United States.

There are seven hundred and sixty-four civilian and military personnel working within FORTEC. Of that seven hundred and sixty-four, an unknown number work in a small area separated from the rest and under a tight security guard. And of that secret number, there is one man in one other, still smaller, building. It is like the last tiny box in a Chinese puzzle.

The man and the building are unique on the entire base. Of all the many persons working at Wright-Patterson, only this man and this building have a security system designed and built specifically for them. Like a ring within a ring, this electronic guardian assures that no one enters and no one leaves, save the man himself. Even then, he can only enter at precisely nine o'clock on Monday morning and leave at five o'clock on Friday evening. There is a time window, when the electronic security system is deactivated for exactly sixty seconds, during which time the door to the small concrete building is automatically unlocked and the man can come or go. Every other hour from nine o'clock Monday to five o'clock Friday, this man spends inside the impregnable structure.

This man is—was—Barney Russom's twin brother.

It took half an hour for Barney and his wife Nancy to drive from South Dayton Airport to the nearby suburb of Kettering. Behind the wheel of the rented car, Barney was taciturn and somber. Nancy was pale, her mind numbed by grief.

Barney turned and looked at Nancy. She was dressed in a dark brown knit suit. Her mahogany eyes matched her hair—a pretty girl, not stunning. Her personality complemented Barney's, and the triangular relationship between herself, Barney, and Bob added to her grief. It was as if Barney himself were now dead. She sat silently and watched the miles peel past as Barney steered the car.

"There's something I wasn't going to tell you until later," Barney said.

"About Bob?"

"Ginger will probably tell you," he said, "but Bob was going to resign his commission and take the job at Stanford."

"Did *he* tell you that?"

Barney nodded. "He sent a letter to the office. We were going to surprise you."

Nancy was quiet and Barney kept his eyes focused on the traffic ahead. After a few more miles, he heard her sobbing again. It had been a long time since he felt so helpless.

Barney said nothing, the ache swelling within him, and they drove the rest of the way in uneasy silence.

How could it be? Barney had asked himself the question over and over on the flight from San Francisco. In the cliché of such fairy-tale success, Bob had "everything in the world." Now he was dead. His wife Ginger was left alone with their tiny daughter. Why? Why did he do it? Why did Robert Russom put the muzzle of a revolver against his temple and pull the trigger, as they had said? Certainly there had been the normal domestic problems, Barney thought again. There had been problems with the Air Force, and his job in the military was severely demanding. But now, after countless discussions with his brother, Bob was about to accept a professorship in Stanford Medical Center's Pathology Department.

Bob had joined the Air Force immediately after graduation, and quickly rose to the rank of captain as a result of his important pathology work in Southeast Asia, probing the effects of jungle infections. After the Far Eastern tour, Captain Robert Russom had spent a few years at Walter Reed Hospital in Washington, D.C., as Assistant to the Director of Pathology. Three years ago he had met Ginger; they were married only weeks later in Arlington, Virginia.

Soon after, he was assigned to Wright-Patterson Air Force Base in a *Case 99* position——the highest possible security clearance. It is here that any detailed history of Robert Russom's work assignment for the Air Force ends. It is known only that his mysterious duties were carried out under the auspices of FORTEC.

Barney was acutely aware now, more than ever, that he was ignorant of exactly what work his brother had been doing. Not even Ginger knew. The thought chewed and tugged at him.

Barney pulled the car into the broad driveway of his brother's home. He and Nancy sat there briefly in stilled silence, unmoving, almost afraid to open the door and step once again into the world of sorrow. A white oak rustled and washed the house in mottled shadows. Strangely, Barney remembered how his dog had reacted last night just before he received the news.

Ginger appeared at the door and rushed to embrace Nancy. Barney became uncomfortable at the sound of the sobbing women and went quickly into the house.

Later, when the women were preparing dinner, Barney went into the living room to examine the contents of Bob's strongbox to see which of his affairs needed immediate attention. For the first time he felt like an intruder into his brother's private life, as he perused the personal documents.

The telephone rang at his elbow and he instinctively picked up the receiver.

"Hello, Mrs. Russom?" the voice said, irritating Barney.

"No, this is her brother-in-law. May *I* help you?"

After a brief pause, the voice continued. "Oh, how do you do. This is Colonel Lowry at Wright-Patterson. I'm the chaplain assigned to handle the funeral arrangements."

"Would you like me to call Mrs. Russom?"

"No, please don't disturb her. I only called to ask if we could send an airman over to pick up a clean uniform for Bob." The chaplain's voice was quiet and deferential.

Barney was silent, the reality of it all slapping him again. "I'm sure that would be all right," he said finally. "I'll be expecting him soon."

Barney went into the master bedroom, not wanting to interrupt the women. He sadly inspected the closet full of clothes and removed the only uniform he saw. It had been worn, but was still clean and pressed.

Barney suddenly stopped himself and stared down at the empty garment, fixing his eyes on the gleaming silver bars. He was stunned to find himself wondering whether the chaplain needed shoes . . . socks . . . underwear.

He removed three pennies and a dime from the trousers, and an empty eyeglass case and two letters from the blue jacket. He stuffed them into his pocket.

Captain Robert Russom was to be interred in Calvary Cemetery, adjacent to Carillon Park on the Great Miami River. The cemetery was large and well kept, encircled by a brick wall five feet high.

The coffin lay on a neat catafalque in a small chapel at the entrance. It was there that Barney could see his brother for the last time. En route, Barney was plagued by the thought of seeing Bob's once-shattered head carefully restored by the clean hands of an anonymous cosmetician. He had grown irritable in the past twelve hours, and Nancy had commented more than once on his nervous, jumpy manner. The sheer emotional turmoil of the sudden loss had even caused a brief outburst at dinner. Barney had broken into tears. He wanted to see Bob one more time.

An expressionless guard stood at parade rest in the morning drizzle. He mechanically snapped his carbine to attention as the mourners approached. The sight of the rifle sent Barney's mind back twelve years to the time he visited the Liberty Bell in Philadelphia. Then, as now, he wondered about the seemingly useless weapons. Would the guard's gun stop anyone strong enough to carry away the Bell? Was one needed to protect a dead man?

Inside, they were greeted by Chaplain Lowry and introduced in quiet courtesy to FORTEC's commanding officer, Colonel Rubin. The coffin was carefully husked with a flag and surrounded by flowers. The dead man's garrison cap lay on the red and white stripes. At the sight of the closed coffin, Nancy gasped and clutched Barney's arm.

Barney stiffened. He whirled instantly, darting his open palm in the direction of the coffin. "What the hell is this?" he demanded loudly, his voice rising. "What the hell is *this?*"

The outburst astonished Nancy and Ginger. The chaplain and Colonel Rubin turned in alarm to Barney.

"Dr. Russom, what do you——"

"It's closed!" Barney shouted. "Open the coffin, goddamn it!"

Barney, pushed over the edge of patience by the impact of his own emotion, moved toward the coffin. Colonel Rubin intercepted him and placed a restraining hand on his shoulder.

"Dr. Russom, of *course* it's closed."

"What do you mean *of course?* I want to *see* my brother!"

"I'm afraid that's impossible, Doctor."

Barney shoved the colonel away roughly and stepped to the catafalque. He whipped away the flag, sending the cap hurtling across a bank of musky gardenias.

"Dr. Russom!"

"Barney, please!"

He didn't hear them. He grabbed the lid of the casket and strained to open it. He heard the dull metallic sound of a lock in a hasp.

"It's locked!" Barney bellowed. "Why the hell is my brother's coffin locked?"

"Dr. Russom," stammered Colonel Rubin, "your brother was a suicide. That's why it's closed. We can't allow you to view the body."

"Don't give me that——" Barney choked, furious.

"But it's standard procedure," the colonel tried to explain. "Don't you understand? Your brother was a *suicide*. No one can *see* the body."

The word *see* jabbed at Barney's anger, and he glared at Rubin with frenzied eyes.

"Then for Christ's sake," he seethed, "why did you want a clean uniform?"

CHAPTER 3

One of Barney Russom's good friends was another scientist, Charlie Blakemore, at forty-one small and thin, almost gaunt. Blakemore's only exercise seemed to be walking alone or turning the pages of books. His only recreation came when he allowed himself the pleasure of calculating the innumerable possibilities and permutations of the Nevada roulette wheels.

The intellectual prowess of the two men led them to form a close relationship with each other—not so much socially, due to Charlie's introversion, but intellectually, in every sense of the word. Charlie worked close to Barney, at Sylmar Electronics, just south of Palo Alto, where he was now Director of the Advanced Systems Laboratory. They often left their respective plants and met at Charlie's beach house to play chess or discuss a new development they had read about in a Physics Society journal.

Blakemore had never married; he lived in near seclusion outside a small village on the coast. He was a singular man. His vision had begun to deteriorate in school, and now he was almost blind. The glasses he wore were almost an inch thick, and made his eyes unduly large when he looked at you directly. Little crescents of intensified light shone on the tops of his cheeks and gave him an odd appearance. His thick black hair was curly and unkempt; his clothes baggy and out of style.

Charlie seldom worked before eleven in the morning. His day was cluttered with a variety of projects ranging from research programs to interviewing young engineers. But sometimes he would be awakened by a

25

new idea in the dark pit of the night. And Charlie was compelled—almost physically forced—to transform his ideas into humming hardware. On such occasions, it was not unusual for the security officers changing shifts at 6 a.m. to receive the message that Blakemore was already at work. Neither Blakemore's secretary nor his co-workers were then surprised to find him twisting the knobs of an oscilloscope while dressed in pajamas and bathrobe. Charlie Blakemore was the only person at Sylmar who was allowed free access to all laboratories and projects regardless of the security involved.

Charlie didn't smoke or drink. His chief diversion from his work at Sylmar was his unusual hobby: Charlie Blakemore bred exotic strains of insects. This interest had begun in school, where his fellow students could not relate this avocation to electronics; Barney had been the only one who would talk to Charlie about his entomological pursuits. They would discuss Charlie's contention that the social behavior of lesser-known species of insects may contribute valuable knowledge to twentieth-century man. In his few spare hours, Charlie had become an expert in biochemistry, and today entomologists throughout the world solicited his counsel.

Years ago Charlie had released the friendship-binding catalyst, borne surreptitiously in a chance remark.

Barney and Charlie were coming from the traffic-ridden frenzy of El Camino Real, when Barney looked up quickly.

"What did you say just then?"

"What do you mean, what did I just say?" Charlie's eyes grew grotesquely larger through the thick glasses.

"About the possibility of insects on other planets," Barney said.

"Well," Charlie said, "I merely pointed out that we may learn something from the organizational patterns and apparent social order of insects. You just mentioned my hobby, and I said the study of the insect colony structure may contribute to our quest for more information on man's survival in severe environments."

"No," Barney went on. "You said something about extraterrestrial life, didn't you?"

The little shiny crescents gleamed on his cheeks as Blakemore kept his eyes on the road, mildly embarrassed. "All I said, Barney, was that there certainly is a possibility that crude life forms may exist outside of Earth. But I would be inclined to believe they would be elementary insect forms, simply because insects are better able to endure reduced pressures and temperature variations. That sort of thing."

"Charlie," Barney said eagerly, "don't be so goddamn pedantic. Do you believe it or not?"

"Well," Charlie said, "insects have interested me for a long time."

"I mean the other thing. Life out there. You believe it, don't you?"

"Well, the possibilities are——"

Barney pressed Charlie. "I haven't told many people this, but I *know* there is life elsewhere in the universe."

Charlie squinted. "How do you *know?* Do you have proof?"

"I think," said Barney, "that soon we may be able to use the theories of radio communication and possibly monitor advanced alien societies, even though we may never be able to respond."

Now it was Charlie's turn to smile. "Eavesdrop on insects?"

"On whatever," Barney said, shrugging.

For many years after that, Charlie Blakemore and Barney Russom frequently discussed the possibilities of extraterrestrial civilizations. This seed of theory was to flourish in the form of mathematical equations and Russom-designed communication instruments. It became Barney's secret obsession to construct a vast array of antennas outside Carson City, Nevada. The flat plain there would grant as much space as he needed for his mammoth project.

After graduation from college, Charlie Blakemore received a Guggenheim Fellowship, allowing him to continue his studies in Italy and to research high-frequency radio theory at the Marconi Institute in Rome. He was there for three years.

Then, after working with the War Department during World War II, he taught for five years at the University of California at Berkeley. Early in 1950 he joined Sylmar Electronics in Massachusetts and was later appointed Chief Designer of the firm's West Coast Development Laboratories. Blakemore was responsible for several significant breakthroughs that had important application in the nation's missile technology.

Later it became Blakemore's charge to head a special team of engineers and scientists who developed security systems for the then secret Minuteman ICBM launch silos. Like invisible fences, the systems set up electromagnetic fields which nothing could penetrate without detection.

The project, known as ELSIE (for Electronic Security and Identification), was so successful that a large continuing contract was granted to Sylmar. The system eventually was employed at major Air Force bases with *Case 99* requirements.

Two days after the burial of his brother, Barney Russom placed a telephone call from San Francisco International Airport to his friend Charlie Blakemore.

"Charlie, you're still an expert in chemistry and biology, right?"

Blakemore was sleepy, but his scientific mind reacted automatically. "Something of an expert. God, Barney, it's eleven-thirty at night!"

"Would you be surprised to see a lot of silicon radicals in a pathology report?"

"In a pathology report?" There was surprise in Charlie's voice.

"That's what I said," Barney answered.

"Silicon? Are you sure they're not *carbon* radicals? They're chemically similar, you know."

Barney's hand gripped the telephone tighter at the other end. Charlie could sense an urgency he had never noticed in his friend's speech.

"No, these are silicates," Barney said. "I recognize them from my work in transistors."

"Barney, what does all this have to do with a pathology report?"

"Nothing, Charlie. That's why I'm calling. I have a pathology report here that's loaded with silicon radicals."

"Are there any carbons in it?" Charlie could hear the rattling of paper and supposed Barney was looking at the report.

"No," Barney said finally. "I don't see any."

"Then it couldn't be a pathology report, Barney," Charlie sighed, the scientist taking over in his manner. "Because the tissue of all living things is based upon carbon, as you should already know. Silicon only occurs occasionally in some nonorganic plants and some animal parts. Like feathers, say."

"I don't know about all that, Charlie. All I know is that I'm holding in my hands a pathology report, and I don't see a single goddamn carbon radical *in* it."

"Where did you get it?" Charlie asked.

"I can't tell you yet, Charlie. But what would your first reaction be?"

"Barney, my first reaction would be that it's simply *not* a pathology report, that's all. It's either a joke or a report on some strange, deep-sea bird—an underwater turkey, Barney."

Charlie then snickered thinly at his remark.

Barney was silent on the other end. One by one, he counted the silicon radicals again. There were thirty-three.

"Why did you say *deep sea?*" Barney asked finally.

Charlie sighed again. "Well, I just meant some place we've never been before, some place we don't know about."

Without saying good-bye to his friend, Barney hung up the telephone and headed for Charlie's cottage.

CHAPTER 4

The day after Barney's clamorous outburst at the burial of his brother, he was scheduled for a board meeting of a small New York bank, another of Barney's business activities. Nancy had decided to stay a few more days with Ginger and the baby.

On the way to the airport, Barney again apologized. "I was just furious at military bureaucracy butting into our own business," he said. "I'm sorry, Nancy, but it just didn't seem right."

"I'm sorry, too," she replied feebly.

"It's bad enough," Barney continued, "that we don't know why he did it, but what bothers me most is why the hell they have to *hide* him from us."

"Barney, I suppose after seeing you fly off the handle so often, I shouldn't be so upset, but please, *please*, let's just drop it."

Hearing the distress in her voice, Barney yielded and changed the subject. "I'll be in New York a couple of days at the most. Nancy, when I get back, let's take a week off and go up to the cabin. It'll do us good. Why don't you ask Ginger to come on out and stay with us for a few months?"

"All right. You'll be sure to call me when you get back home?"

Barney agreed.

Aboard a 727 on Flight 265 for Kennedy Airport, Barney tried to relax over his Scotch. The last three days had seemed endless, yet at thirty thousand feet they were remote and distant. The steady whine of the engines seemed to mesmerize him as he stared out the

31

window at the frosty patchwork of white and dark green farmlands.

A stewardess distributed magazines and asked Barney if he would enjoy another drink. He shook his head without turning from the window. His hands, holding the small cruet and glass, rested on his leather briefcase; small wet circles of condensation appeared on the smooth, brown surface.

Barney unfolded the plastic table from the back of the seat and put the drink on it. Then he idly opened his briefcase, thinking that another reading of his forthcoming address would occupy his mind for the remainder of the flight.

He noticed the two envelopes he had taken from his brother's uniform, and sadly gazed at them as he took the last of his drink. He wished the stewardess would return.

Picking up the two envelopes, Barney noticed that one was not addressed. It was a plain white envelope whose slim bulk told him it held a letter. The other was a thick, long manila envelope, addressed to Bob and bearing an Oslo, Norway, postmark. The return address indicated the sender was with the Department of Pathology at the University of Oslo. He opened the smaller envelope first.

Dear Ginger,

I don't know why I'm writing this. I'm just lonely, and even though it's only Tuesday, I find the days getting longer and longer. Every time they lock the door behind me on Monday morning, it seems that Friday is a year away.

By the way, that was a splendid dinner you cooked for the Martins Saturday evening. Sorry I had too much of that wine because I know you've been worried about my relationship with "the sauce" lately.

I've got to get out of here, honey. These things are driving me further and further away from reality. Every time I think how happy Barney was about my getting out of the service, I become more and more impatient. How will you feel about living in Palo Alto with an underpaid pathologist?

We'll be close to Barney and Nancy and Janet will be able to see her uncle more often. I'll bet

The last word hung before Barney's eyes and he turned the page over to find more. There was nothing. He checked the envelope again. Barney reread the letter and then put it into his pocket. He sensed something bizarre about the letter and it bothered him. But he didn't know why.

He opened the manila envelope and removed a two-page form filled with chemical symbols and equations, along with a covering letter. After scanning the form, he read the letter.

My dear Captain Russom:

There must be some mistake. The sample you forwarded us for analysis has been checked carefully and does not conform to present scientific disciplines. We suspect that perhaps you inadvertently sent the wrong sample, and we invite you to send the intended specimen along at your convenience.

However, in the interests of whatever use it may serve, we are including our results on the sample we did receive. You'll note immediately that this sample only resembles organic tissue as we know it in the fact that silicon has replaced the normal hydrocarbon chains.

If you'll allow me a small joke, sir, this sample seems to be merely part of a child's toy, or what even the Norwegian children are calling "silly putty."

All of us here at the laboratory await with interest the arrival of the tissue sample mentioned in your letter. As usual, a copy of this report has gone to the Board of Inquiry.

I remain,

Very truly yours,
V. Ingmar Haggard, M.D.
Department of Pathology

Barney frowned and looked at the other pages. He glanced over the series of equations and noted the familiar chemical symbols. He determined to call Charlie Blakemore immediately when he got back to San Francisco. He was baffled by the notations on what appeared to be an official pathology report form.

It had just begun to snow when Barney arrived at the Essex House in Manhattan. A nearby theater was showing a movie he wanted to see, and he promised himself a few hours' relaxation that evening. The desk clerk recognized him, as he did all the Pace International people, and greeted him warmly.

"It's good to see you again, Dr. Russom. We have your usual room available. How long do you plan to be with us?"

"Just a day or so this time. I'll be back for the I-Triple-E convention," Barney said, nodding at the smaller man.

"By the way, Doctor, there are some messages for you." The clerk took two folded pages from the pigeon-hole behind him.

In the elevator, Barney read the first note. Norman Fine of *Electronics Week* wanted to speak with him.

"That pest has hunted me down," Barney said aloud.

"I beg your pardon, sir?" the bellboy said.

Barney waved him off impatiently. "Nothing."

The other message was to telephone his wife. In his room Barney dismissed the bellboy, thrusting a dollar into his hand. He took off his jacket and tie, then sprawled across the bed, kicking off his shoes.

A few moments later, Nancy's familiar voice told him the maid had called from Palo Alto to say a telegram had arrived for him.

"Someone in New York has canceled your seminar speech for the convention," Nancy said.

*"Can*celed?"

"They didn't give any reason. They said a detailed letter would follow, but I thought you'd want to know while you're there."

"I know who probably sent it. I'll call him while I'm here. How's Ginger holding up?"

"She's doing fine," Nancy said. "I asked her about coming out to stay with us for a while and she'd like to. Oh, that Colonel Rubin called and told Ginger she's going to get full insurance payments. He said the Air Force is making a special exception in Bob's case."

Barney was angered at the news. Thanks a hell of a lot, he thought, but he didn't pursue it, not wanting to distress Nancy. He said, "That'll be good for Ginger. I'll be home day after tomorrow. Give Turp an extra biscuit for me."

"You and that dog!" It was the first light note he'd heard in her voice in days.

"And don't forget about the week at the lake." Barney knew he didn't have to say more.

He waited before touching the telephone again. It wasn't taking much these days to bounce him into irrational anger. Now the sugar-covered placebo of money offered by the Air Force chafed at him. He waited for his resentment to cool.

Next he placed a call to Nathan Eldridge of Omega Semiconductor in Northampton, Long Island. Eldridge headed the program committee for the convention and had been the one who invited Barney to organize a special seminar.

"I'm sorry," the syrupy voice of Eldridge's secretary said. "He's in a meeting now, sir. May I take a message?"

Barney's voice remained controlled as his irritation returned. "No, you may not. This is Dr. Russom of Pace International, and I'd like you to get him out of the meeting."

"I can't do that, Dr. Russom."

"Get him out," Barney commanded. "I want to talk to him and it can't wait."

"Just a moment, sir," the flustered girl said. "I'll see if I can get him."

Barney rolled over on his back and glared impatiently at the yellow, cracked ceiling. He loosened his belt, thinking that it was a pretty crummy room for twenty-five dollars a day.

The secretary came back on the line. "Mr. Eldridge said he can't come to the phone right now, sir, but he promises to call you back in fifteen minutes."

"I'm at the Essex House," Barney said rudely, and hung up.

It then occurred to him that he hadn't eaten, and the Scotch on the plane had brought on his mild gastritis. He picked up the telephone again and asked for room service.

"What kind of soup do you have?"

A heavily accented voice informed him that he could have clear bouillion, vichysoisse, or potage d'épinards.

"What's that?"

The haughty voice replied, "Sir, it's cream of spinach."

What Barney really wanted was some of Nancy's hearty soup, but the cream of spinach would have to do. "And some milk," he said. "And some crackers."

He stripped to his shorts and turned on the television set. A skinny man with a mustache was giving the weather forecast. Barney sat on a chair and waited for Eldridge's call.

The knock at the door was followed by a crisp "Room Service."

"Come in," he called.

Three smartly uniformed waiters entered, pushing a long linen-covered table. Barney remembered he was only in his shorts. "Just leave it," he said. "Thank you."

"But *monsieur*," the tallest waiter insisted, "we would enjoy serving you."

God! Barney thought. It's all over the place! Nobody does anything simply any more. "Give me the goddamn check," he said. Then he thrust the check with the pencil-scrawled BMR at the nearest waiter.

As they were leaving, the telephone rang.

"Barney?" It was Nathan Eldridge returning his call.

Without the amenities, Barney said, "My seminar was canceled. Do you know anything about it?"

"I'm afraid I do, Barney. The committee has given it further consideration and——"

"Come on, Nathan. Why was it canceled?"

"Well, I . . . I don't know for sure, Barney, but I think it's probably a couple of things. First of all, you've been scooped by *Aviation and Space Management* magazine. In today's issue they just published a twelve-page article attributing the UFO phenomena to ball lightning and simple plasma emissions from power lines."

"What? I haven't seen it. Besides, how the hell could they have *scooped* me? My discussion was to explore the possibility of these things being *real,* for crissakes."

The voice at the other end suddenly became cool and distant. "Barney," it said, "I must tell you also that the other thing was the Air Force putting a little of their familiar pressure on us. They're sick and tired of being criticized for holding off on giving out any UFO information, you know. You know they have let that contract for three hundred thousand dollars to the University of Colorado, to square the whole thing away. So, in light of these two new developments, the committee decided your discussion was inappropriate at this time."

"The committee decided, or the Air Force decided?" Barney asked gruffly.

"Barney, as an employee of Omega and as head of this committee, I had no choice. I'm sure you understand."

"I understand Omega's *marketing* problems, if that's what you mean, Nathan, but——"

"Now, Barney, don't get upset."

"Upset? Why the hell don't you give the goddamn

magazine a seminar of its own? You know goddamn well the Air Force owns every editor on it!"

"Well, I'm afraid it's out of my hands now, Barney."

"Who are you going to replace me with?"

"Dr. Melchior of ETT Corporation is going to conduct a seminar on hot carrier diodes."

Barney shook his head in disbelief and looked at the ceiling. "You phony bastards," he said. Then he saw his soup getting cold in its dull pewter urn, seeming anachronistic in this age of space travel and computers.

"I guess there's nothing more to say, Nathan." Barney slammed down the receiver and went over to the table. "Hot carrier diodes," he murmured. "Jesus H. Christ." The soup was cold. He didn't want it anyway.

CHAPTER 5

Washington, D. C., was one of Barney's favorite cities. He enjoyed the four-hour drive from New York along the Garden State Thruway, even though it took him through the smoky blotch of Baltimore, which scarred the placid white scenery like a greasy stain on a Currier and Ives print.

There is a small, quiet tavern facing DuPont Circle on Connecticut Avenue. It was here that Barney had arranged to meet one of his oldest friends, Brigadier General Joseph S. Quinting. Quinting was Assistant Chief of Foreign Intelligence at the Pentagon, second in command to someone Barney knew only as "Teddyrook."

Joe Quinting was the third youngest general in the Air Force, having received his star six months ago, one day before his fortieth birthday. He held a degree in engineering and an M.B.A. from Princeton. He had achieved the status of ace in the last year of World War II and that of triple ace in Korea. He had two years as a test pilot between World War II and Korea, developing North American's F-86 fighter. After Korea he was assigned as liaison between industry and the Air Force for industry procurement. Since then he had been with military intelligence. His dedication to his Air Force career, his many decorations, and his professional credentials had quickly boosted him to the rank of colonel. He was indeed the fair-haired boy of Air Force Intelligence, although it was Quinting's lot to receive the dirtiest and most distasteful of military chores. Fortunately, Quinting was a bachelor. Self-assured and confident, he never questioned the importance of any job he attacked, nor did he have the slightest doubt that he could accomplish any mission successfully. Quinting in uniform was electric; obedience was a foregone conclusion when the man with the gleaming white teeth and the panatella cigar assuredly and in soft tones gave an order.

Barney had known Joe since he, Bob, and Quinting were boys in California. During Quinting's tenure as procurement officer, he and Barney often had business contact, and both relished the frequent opportunities to share blue-jeaned memories of frog-jumping contests, late-night double dating, and clandestine conclaves in secret caves.

Barney had called his friend the night before and arranged to meet him for a drink at five-thirty. Quinting, dressed in a dark blue business suit, was seated at the bar when Barney entered. Barney had almost forgotten the familiar panatella that was invariably affixed to Joe's mouth. It was as much a part of him as his perpetual grin. Quinting was dark; his angular features framed his deep eyes and his hair was full and black.

The cigar remained clenched between Joe's teeth as he greeted Barney. "I'll be goddamned if you don't get heavier every time I see you, you bastard," Joe beamed. He grabbed Barney's outstretched hand and pressed it warmly. "Are you and your company still sucking the government's tit every time you invent something we can't possibly do without?"

Barney laughed and slapped his friend's shoulder. "Better than being such obvious free-loaders as you fly-boys. At least we say please."

Quinting removed the panatella from his teeth and regarded Barney soberly. "Listen, pal," he said, "I'll only say this once and then we'll forget it. I just heard the news about Bob yesterday. Didn't want to mention it when you called. I'm sorry as hell, Barney. I wasn't as close to him as I am to you. But I'm sorry as hell."

Barney nodded, understanding Joe's sympathy. It was all Joe could say.

"And now," Joe continued, "since I don't want to

pay for these things all evening, I'll let the rich business executive buy the horny General a drink."

"All right," Barney laughed. "After all, it's *your* money."

Barney ordered the drinks and took Joe's arm. "Let's go over to that corner booth. I don't think I'm going to be in a good mood for very long."

"I hope *that* won't last," Quinting said as they moved to the booth. "You're coming over to have dinner with Maggie and me, aren't you?"

"How *is* she, Joe?" Barney asked. "Still putting up with you?"

Quinting flicked ashes with studied casualness, and looked at Barney. "Time for another marriage sermon?"

"I've given up on that," Barney shrugged. "But one of these days you're going to lose her."

Quinting sighed. "Maybe you're right, pal. But I can't ask this gal to marry a guy who'll be home only two nights a week."

"But you're only with her two nights a week, anyway, Joe. What's the difference?"

Quinting refused to consider the subject. "You know how fantastic she is, Barney. Two nights is all I can take. Listen, she's really looking forward to seeing you tonight. I told her you were coming."

Barney shook his head. "Can't do it, Joe. I'm flying back to San Francisco at eight tonight."

"You're kidding! I phoned Maggie and told her to lay out some lasagna and some booze."

"Look, I'll be back for the convention in three weeks. Let me take you up on it then. Right now I want to ask you a big favor."

The waiter brought them a Scotch-over and a Tanqueray martini. Barney paid him, and when the man left, he looked at his friend.

"What's the favor?" Joe asked.

"It may mean breaking the rules, Joe. Knowing the Air Force, the matter has probably been classified." Barney pulled at the Scotch.

"Well, I have to be careful," Joe said, "but go ahead. What's the favor?"

"Some biggy in the Air Force apparently had a forthcoming seminar of mine canceled."

"What was it about?"

"UFO's," Barney said evenly.

Joe sucked on his cigar. The years of training clicked on a warning light in his mind. Whenever possible, he tried not to think of the subject. "That's a hell of a touchy subject around here right now, Barney. We've been taking a lot of criticism from every nut in the country about it."

"Including me?" Barney asked.

Joe shook his head. "Nah, not you. At least you have some scientific basis for your wild theories. Is that what you were going to talk about?"

Barney nodded. "Right. I was going to explain in detail how there might very well *be* something to it all."

"Same old Barney," Joe laughed.

"I was even going to jab the Air Force a bit," Barney went on.

"That's not unusual, but maybe they didn't like the way you were going to jab them."

"That's just it, Joe. No one has even seen the contents of the paper. Not even *Nancy,* for crissakes." Barney tapped lightly on the table top.

"Well, didn't your committee know? Don't they have to okay everything?"

"All they got was a précis of the speech," Barney replied. "They knew nothing of my actual address."

Joe shrugged. "Are you sure *we* shot you down?" he asked.

"That's what I was told."

"What do you want me to do?"

"Find out for me why the hell they canceled it without even knowing what I was going to say." Barney's voice grew firm.

"Well, you know, Barney," Joe went on, "Project Blue Book handles the flying saucer stuff and it's not under my wing. It's handled directly from the Foreign

Technology Division at Wright-Patterson." The warning light grew brighter.

Barney's expression became distant and passive. He looked at Joe without seeing him. His thoughts left the room.

Joe jokingly passed his hand in front of Barney's eyes. "Barney? You still with me, pal?"

"Joe," Barney said pensively. "Bob was attached to FORTEC. Don't you have something to do with them, too?"

"Hell, there's your reason," Joe said, ignoring Barney's question. "They probably deferred the seminar to save you any discomfort. Sometimes we *do* think of the other guy, you know." Joe smiled again and took another drag on the cigar.

"Well," Barney said finally. "If you could do anything, you know how much I'd appreciate it."

"I think that's the reason, but I'll ask around for you." Joe plinked his empty glass. "But it's going to cost you, pal. How about another drink?"

Barney motioned the waiter for another round. Then he added, "Say, Joe, what do you know about pension things? You know, insurance crap and all that."

"Oh, a little, I guess. Why?"

"Small matter, really. It seems like *everything* is bothering me these days."

Joe looked at him and frowned. "What's *this* about?"

"As you may have heard, Bob shot himself. Or at least that's what they said he did. We never did get to see the body."

Joe nodded.

"But Nancy called me from Ohio yesterday and said Ginger would be getting full-benefit payments. They made an exception for some reason in Bob's case and they're treating it like a regular accident."

Joe's eyes lit up. "Wow," he said. "That's pretty fancy. What was he doing for FORTEC, anyway?"

Barney shook his head. "I haven't the vaguest idea. Not even Ginger knew." Then, "I thought since you were attached to FORTEC, you could find out what's going on."

"Well, if it's any comfort to you, not even Maggie knows what *I* do, either. FORTEC is a pretty razzle-dazzle operation, pal." Joe grinned again. "But I'll see what I can do."

"Good. Could you call me at my place tomorrow?" Barney asked.

"Hold on, now. Calm down. I need a little time."

"Joe, I know you've got connections. Can't you phone me tomorrow? I just want to know about those two things."

"Okay," Joe answered in mock surrender. "Pick a time because I'll have to give you the poop from a pay phone. Every telephone in the Pentagon is bugged now, and I even suspect the spooks from the CIA have our apartment phone tapped." Joe then tossed off the rest of his new drink.

"About five-thirty. I'll be waiting."

Joe nodded, puffing the panatella. "Okay, I'll call you then."

They ordered a third drink and chatted for a few more minutes about Barney's work at Pace International. Then Barney remembered Nathan Eldridge's comments. "Hey, by the way, Joe. You Air Force guys read *Aviation and Space Management* magazine, don't you?"

"Sometimes, yeah," Joe replied.

"There was an article this morning on UFO's. Did you see it?"

"No," Joe said, "but I heard about it at lunch today. Sounds like hot stuff."

"What do you think?" Barney asked.

"You mean as a G-2 or as a friend of yours?"

"Either way," Barney said.

"Well, I have very little information on what the article actually said, but I'd bet you a month's salary it's a plant by the Blue Book boys."

After returning to San Francisco and calling Charlie Blakemore, Barney went directly to Charlie's cottage on the coast. The flight from Washington was used mostly for much-needed sleep, but Barney also went over the article Nathan Eldridge had mentioned. He was furious, and circled numerous statements with a red pencil, deciding to point out the inconsistencies in the story with a letter to the magazine's editor.

It was foggy at the cottage and well past midnight when Barney arrived. He knocked harshly on the door, and a light went on. Charlie opened the door.

"Why didn't you say you were coming out instead of just hanging up?"

"Sorry, Charlie, but I want you to look at this thing."

"Let me have it," Charlie said, taking the manila envelope from Barney.

Barney followed him into a small room that served as a chemistry lab, which Charlie had stocked to aid him in his study of insects.

"Oslo, eh?" Charlie said finally. "Professor Haggard is perhaps the world's foremost pathologist. I see he still has that sense of humor with this 'silly putty' stuff." Blakemore looked up and snorted in amusement, but went back to the report when he saw no reaction from Barney.

Barney paced the room while Blakemore drew figures on scraps of yellow paper. He toyed with his thick glasses and looked up occasionally, thinking. It was as though Barney weren't there.

Thirty minutes later Blakemore called from the desk. "Odd" was his first word, and Barney's pulse jumped.

"What do you think?" Barney asked excitedly.

"This is apparently a very exotic material, Barney. It's possible to reconstruct a chemical model of the specimen, even though no specific test was called for. If I know Professor Haggard, he probably went through the entire analysis, whether he thought it was 'silly putty' or not."

"Can you identify the specimen?" Barney asked.

"Well," Charlie went on pedantically, "silicon is found almost everywhere, as you should know. The structure of this sample is based primarily on silicates. All organic things, including you and me, are based upon the element of carbon, rather than silicon, even though silicon is occasionally found in nonorganic matter. I mentioned that before, I think. What puzzles me, though, is that this sample seems to resemble animal tissue in every way except for the absence of hydrocarbons so necessary to life. It's as if you took normal human tissue and replaced the carbon with silicon."

Barney's voice was low. "Does that mean there could be an organism somewhere whose physiological foundations are silicate?"

Charlie adjusted his glasses and squinted up at Barney. "My dear friend," he said, recalling to Barney how ludicrous many people thought Charlie's serious approach was, "it is you and I who are the odd ones. A carbon base for our own makeup is far from being the most logical and, indeed, the most probable cell structure. I know it's been a long time since you took chemistry, but you certainly should remember that next to oxygen, silicon is the most abundant element in the universe."

Barney picked up the report from his friend's desk and walked back to the living room. He put on his coat. "I'm sorry I kept you up, Charlie."

"What on earth was Bob doing with this stuff, anyway?"

Barney opened the front door and turned to Charlie.

"I'm more concerned," he said evenly, "with what this stuff, as you call it, was doing with *him*."

CHAPTER 6

At five-thirty the next evening, Barney went into his study and closed the door.

At the same time, General Joseph S. Quinting pulled his car into a service station in Arlington, Virginia. After one bad connection and a brief argument with the operator, the call went through.

"Can you hear me all right now, Joe?" Barney's voice was clear.

"I wish you guys would devote some time to the telephone company instead of always kissing it up at the Cape."

"What did you find out?" Barney was anxious.

"It looks like you were right," Joe said. "They didn't want any more pressure on them about saucers, particularly in front of eighty thousand engineers in New York and a jillion trade journal readers."

"That's the only reason?"

"Looks like it. One other thing. Did you know that the editor of *Aviation and Space Management* was at Wright-Patterson last week? It had to be cleared with my office, but I didn't remember it yesterday."

"Those bastards," Barney said. "I didn't think they could get that petty."

"Another thing," Joe said. "We gave Colorado University a fat contract to look into the UFO thing to get the nuts off our back. Until the results are in, you probably won't hear an official Air Force word about anything that flies over five miles."

"Well, thanks, Joe. I appreciate your help." The news eased his anger only a little.

"Oh," Joe cut in, "I have something on the other

matter, too. Nobody seems to know why, but Bob's wife *is* going to get full insurance benefits. And that's pretty damned rare."

"I thought it was," Barney said.

"You're damn right! So unusual that it's only happened eight times since Korea. And four of them in the last six months." Joe paused briefly. "But they were all members of the same flight crew, which could account for it."

Barney sat upright in his chair. "Joe," he said quietly, "does it say where their plane was based?"

Barney heard the shuffling of papers at the other end. "Jesus jumping Christ!"

The ridge of Barney's wedding band cut into his finger as he gripped the telephone. "What's the matter?"

"I just noticed. They were an air evacuation crew based at Wright-Patterson."

"Joe," Barney said, "I may just be dreaming or crazy or something, but everything seems to be connected, and I don't know why."

Quinting was puzzled at Barney's reaction. "Connected with what?"

Barney went on, "Can you get me the names of those four men?"

"What the hell are you trying to do? Force my retirement?"

"No, I mean it. Can you get their names and addresses?"

"Will you get off my ass, then?" Joe said in the irritated tone one could use only with friends.

"Can you call me back at this time tomorrow?"

"Yeah, but after that, it'll have to be postcards. It's not like I was in public relations, you know. I've got to split now."

"So long," Barney said. "And thanks, Joe."

"Forget it, pal. Keep calm. My advice is to take a few days off. Go someplace."

With that Joe Quinting chuckled good-naturedly and hung up. Barney was already cradling his own telephone and reaching for his drink.

He sat for a long while in the quiet study, aching, staring across the room. His eyes turned to a tarnished swimming trophy, and the knot of emotion began to draw tighter.

A soft scratching at the door broke his reverie, and Turpin nosed his way through the opening. "Hi, boy," Barney said dejectedly. "I guess everyone's been ignoring you lately. You getting enough to eat?"

The dog nuzzled Barney with his cold snout, and the man patted the animal's breast affectionately. "I wonder if you know how lucky you are, Turp," he said, "having all four feet on the ground and seeing everything with double vision. Everyone around you has only one foot down firm and can't see beyond the end of his nose. Wish you could help me now."

The dog regarded him quizzically, tilting his head and poking Barney with his nose, as if pondering his master's comments.

Barney stood up. "How about a walk, Turp? The fresh air might do us good."

With that, the dog ran through the doorway ahead of him. Barney picked up his jacket and the dog's leash and switched off the lights in his study.

The crisp night air cut through Barney's dusty mind as he and Turpin walked slowly down a poorly lighted road toward downtown. They passed a couple necking in a parked car, and a block later, a noisy party.

It was almost ten-thirty when Barney crossed El Camino Real in downtown Palo Alto. The marquee of the movie house announced the same film he had planned to see in New York. He never did get the needed relaxation. As he walked, his thoughts were disjointed and the chilling night air snapped at his body under the thin jacket. He went into a small coffee shop and tied Turp just inside the doorway. Barney seated himself heavily in a booth and ordered coffee.

When the waitress set the chipped mug in front of him, he stirred the coffee slowly and stared into its streaming depths. He allowed his thoughts to speak to him.

For God's sake, Russom, you're a scientist. All

these things that have been bothering you lately have a definite place in a logical scheme. You won't get the answers by attacking them emotionally. You can program a computer in Fortran-2. You can work a partial differential equation almost mentally. If you think there's a problem here, try to work it out as a scientist. Write the facts down. Let them speak for themselves. Judge them independently. Then . . . then, see if there's a relationship.

Barney's hand groped through his pockets for a scrap of paper. He found a small stub of a pencil and pulled out the blank white envelope containing his brother's letter to Ginger. He had almost forgotten about it. Now he read it for the fourth time. What was wrong with it? What bothered him so much about it? It sounded as if Bob was depressed. Certainly, having to stay in his secret laboratory for an entire week and only seeing his family on weekends was tough, but he only had a few months to go. He hadn't sounded unhappy in his letter to me, Barney thought, but he did say he was looking forward to leaving the service and living in California.

The letter obviously had been written after he decided to take the Stanford post. Maybe he was nervous about the new job at Stanford or upset at not seeing Ginger very much. He mentions drinking. Well, hell—it could hurt a marriage or get a man fired, but not drive him to suicide. He says he has to get out of there. Maybe he was mentally disturbed. He talks about straying from reality, about all these things taunting him.

Barney caught himself and read the sentence again.

I've got to get out of here, honey. These things are driving me further and further away from reality.

What things? Barney slammed down his open palm

and said, "Christ! I don't even know what he was *doing!*"

The outburst drew a quick glance from the waitress, and two young girls at the end of the counter giggled.

"More coffee, sir?" the waitress called from behind the counter.

Barney looked at her, embarrassed. "Uh . . . yes. Yes, please. This has gotten cold."

A list! I'll make that list, he thought. On the back of the envelope he penciled:

1. Suicide.
2. Clean uniform. Why?
3. Locked casket.
4. Bob's work—what?
5. Air Force? Seminar?
6. Pathology stuff? Silly putty in Norway?
7. Insurance benefits—rare when suicide.
8. Other four crewmen. Connection at W-P?

Barney looked at the list and thought about a book he used to fool with in school, the *Collected Works of Lewis Carroll*. Barney would search through the last pages of the volume, working out symbolic logic problems and complex syllogisms. What color was the monkey's house? Who smoked Camels? Which car belonged to Sam?

What was Bob doing?

Barney Russom didn't return home until three in the morning. Later, trying to recall that night, he realized he had no idea of where he had wandered. All he knew was that he returned with a list penciled on the back of a white envelope and an important decision.

Barney was going to find the answer, no matter how long it took.

CHAPTER 7

"Are you out of your goddamn mind, Barney?" Joe Quinting's voice crackled over the wries. "Call their *families?*"

"Why not? I want to find out when they all died and maybe get to the bottom of this. We don't even know *how* they died, do we?"

"Barney, listen," Joe said, more evenly this time. "Listen, pal, I've given you privileged information already, and it's *my* ass on the block if something happens, not yours."

"Don't worry, Joe," Barney insisted. "I'll keep you out of it. All I want to do is find out why my brother killed himself and why his wife is getting double indemnity or whatever it is." There was a pressing tone in Barney's voice.

After a short silence, Quinting said, "Barney, I'm telling you straight off, you could get both of us into a hell of a lot of trouble. What good is that information going to do you?"

"It's just something I have to find out," Barney said. "You have my word. I'll keep you out of it. I think there's a connection, that's all. Thanks for the names, Joe."

"Hell, don't thank me, pal. Just write me once in a while care of A. P. O., Leavenworth." With that, Joe Quinting hung up. The light of the alarm grew hot in the back of his mind, but he let his long friendship with Barney insulate him.

Barney looked again at the list of four names with "last-known address" penciled next to them. He picked up the telephone. He asked the operator to get him

Mrs. Morton McKeever of 109 Farnsworth Road, Benton Harbor, Michigan. Several moments later, he was on the line.

"Mrs. McKeever, my name is Dr. Bernard Russom. It's very important to me that I ask you something about your husband."

"Why?" the voice was skeptical. "Did you know Morton?"

"No, but my brother did," he lied. "They were together at Wright-Patterson Air Force Base, and my brother was killed also."

There was a brief silence at the other end. Then, "What do you want to know?"

"Just two things, Mrs. McKeever. How and when did Morton die?"

There was another pause, then the woman's voice spoke in a lowered tone. "It was on September twelfth. His car went out of control on the turnpike. The insurance people said his brakes didn't work."

"Just one more question, please," Barney said, his voice pleading in simulated reverence. "Did this happen near Wright-Patterson?"

"Oh, no," the woman said. "Morton had a week's leave because he had just returned from a long flight. He was a pilot, you know."

"Yes, I know," Barney lied again. "Thank you very much, Mrs. McKeever. Good-bye."

Barney wrote next to McKeever's name "car accident, September 12th." Then he picked up the telephone again. It was thirty minutes before he was connected with the proper party.

"Is Mrs. Perilli there?"

"No, she's at the movies. Can I take a message?" It was the voice of a young man.

"My name is Dr. Bernard Russom. I'm calling from San Francisco, and it's important that I speak to someone about Stephen Perilli."

"I'm sorry, sir. My brother passed away last year."

"I know," Barney said courteously. "I'm trying to find out when and how he died, because my brother knew him," he added, hoping the flimsy excuse would satisfy the young man.

"It was in a car crash around Labor Day. I think the twelfth of September. Yes, that's right, because he got back from Norway on the tenth."

Barney tensed and wrote the date and cause of death next to the man's name.

Norway!

Barney thanked him and hung up. There were two more names.

The third number he tried to get was the family of Corporal James King in Opelika, Alabama. The family had moved without leaving a forwarding address, but when Barney pressed the operator further, she succeeded in putting him through to a neighbor. A hesitating Southern drawl told him that young Corporal King had died on September twelfth in a car collision a few miles from his home. He was on a week's leave after returning from a trip to Oslo, Norway.

"My God!" Barney shuddered at the neighbor's words. "My good God!" He hung up immediately.

The fourth call was the same. A pharmacist in Los Angeles told Barney that his son was killed on the Santa Ana Freeway on September twelfth of the preceding year.

Barney had his information.

He studied his notes, and his actions grew more frenzied as he paced his study, slamming a clenched fist into his open palm. Sweat beaded on his reddened brow.

Norway. Oslo, Norway.

They all perished in automobile accidents. They all died on the same day. Accidental deaths, so what's so wrong about Joe saying they got full-benefit payments? What's so "rare" about that? But isn't it odd that they *did* all die on the same day? That they just *happened* to be members of the flight crew that just *happened* to have returned from Norway? Which just *happens* to come up every place I turn. Goddammit! Accidents, hell! Who *killed* them? *And is Bob really dead?*

Barney sat down and poured himself a drink. His legs ached, and he could feel his heart pounding.

"Bob's pathology report!" he said aloud. "Everything is Oslo!"

He spent the next three hours pondering it. The blackboard in his head was a Moebius strip. The line of logic traced on the single surface always came back and met itself. A finger tracing its edges always returned to his source. That point was Oslo, Norway.

Barney spent the next day in San Francisco, poring over a week's issues of Norwegian newspapers at the consulate on Post Street. Although they thought the request strange, they brought out from their files the major Oslo newspaper for a few days before and after the previous Labor Day. They also graciously gave him the services of a translator. At noon Barney took the translator to lunch, apologizing once again for the undue strain on the man's throat, and explaining a fabricated project as the reason for the research.

At three-thirty the translator finished reading a story that made Barney react. He asked the man to read it again. The third time, Barney scribbled frantically along with him.

He thanked the consulate people again, gave the translator a generous gratuity, and raced back to Palo Alto with the neatly folded sheet of paper in his breast pocket.

His study was plastered with dozens of sheets of paper: his seminar speech, papers with merely one felt-pen scrawled sentence such as "clean uniform for locked casket," the pathology report, his brother's letters, his notes on the dead flight crew, the pages of the magazine article.

He pinned the scrawled story on a small corkboard panel that he used to tack up newspaper clippings and memos. The release was from *The Stuttgarter Tageblatt,* published in Oslo, Norway.

Oslo, Norway, September 4—Only now a Board of Inquiry of the Norwegian General Staff is preparing publication of a report on the examination of the remains of a UFO which crashed near Spitzbergen, presumably early in the year. Chairman of the Board, Col. Gernod Darnbyl, during an instruction for Air Force officers, stated: "The crashing of the Spitzbergen disc was highly important. Although our present scientific knowledge does not permit us to solve all the riddles, I am confident that these remains from Spitzbergen will be of utmost importance in this respect. Sometime also a misunderstanding was caused by saying that this disc probably was of Soviet origin. *It has—this we wish to state emphatically— not been built by any country on Earth.* The materials used in its construction are completely unknown to all experts who participated in the investigation."

According to Col. Darnbyl, the Board of Inquiry is not going to publish an extensive report "until some sensational facts" have been discussed with United States and British experts. We should reveal what we found out, as misplaced secrecy might lead to panic.

Contrary to information from American and other sources, Second Lieutenants Brobs and Tyllensen, who have been assigned as special observers of the Arctic regions since the event at Spitzbergen, report that flying discs have landed in the polar regions several times. Said Lieutenant Tyllensen, "I think that the Arctic is serving as a kind of air base for the unknown, especially during snowstorms, when we are forced back to our base. I have seen them land and take off on three separate occasions. I notice that, after having landed, they execute a speedy rotation around their discs. A brilliant glow of light, the intensity of which is variable with regard to speed of landing and take-off, prevents any view of the things happening behind this curtain of light and on, or inside, the disc itself."

Barney read the release twice. His hands were trembling as he noted with chilled excitement that the release date was only eight days before the crew met their deaths. Met their deaths after a flight from Oslo, Norway, to Wright-Patterson Air Force Base.

Barney Russom's mind raced back to his seminar paper on UFO's, and in a split second he was reading a book he had used for some material. He was going to point out a rumor recently uncovered by a UFO investigator named John G. Fuller. Now the quotation from the book leaped from the pages and assaulted him with as appalling and frightening a confirmation as any man could come across:

"There have been, I learned after I started this research, frequent and continual rumors (and they are only rumors) that in a morgue at Wright-Patterson Field, Dayton, Ohio, lie the bodies of a half dozen or so small humanoid corpses, measuring not more than four and a half feet in height, evidence of one of the few times an extraterrestrial spaceship has allowed itself either to fail or otherwise fall into the clutches of the semicivilized earth people."

Barney looked at the words, synopsizing the paragraph.

In a morgue at Wright-Patterson Field lie the bodies of a half dozen small humanoid corpses.

He didn't bother to wonder whether the rumor was true. The existence of such humanoid corpses would be the only possible explanation, after the events of the past few days, for the shroud of mystery behind his brother's death . . . for the sudden cancellation of his probing seminar . . . for the strangely coincidental deaths of the four airmen . . . for locking a pathologist in a small, highly secure building for entire weeks.

The humanoid corpses. . . .

Barney realized, too, that the confirmation of such an existence would throw open the technological capabilities of the entire world to an investigation almost cataclysmic in scope—an investigation Barney, for most of his thirty-eight years, had hoped, almost prayed, would occur in his lifetime.

The humanoid corpses. . . .

Barney Russom decided to get one.

CHAPTER 8

The president of Pace International didn't bother to greet Barney's secretary. He walked by her desk in stern silence and closed the door of Barney's office without a word.

Marshall Pace had salt-and-pepper crew-cut hair and was short of stature. He, more than Barney, was responsible for the company's phenomenal growth. While Barney worked long hours over the drawing board and spent interminable hours in the lab with designers and researchers, Pace anxiously watched the movements of the market and always looked as if he were pondering what to say in the next annual report. The corporate problems of P-I were continually on his shoulders, as they had been since he and Barney first formed the company and Barney had designed their original radar-command module. Now it was beginning to show.

Barney was on the phone and didn't look up. Pace plopped himself down on Barney's couch and regarded his associate with affectionate concern. He watched as Barney played nervously with a lucite ball in which was encased the first integrated circuit made by P-I's newly formed microminiaturization facility.

"Okay, Charlie," Barney was saying as he finally looked up and saw Pace. "I can't tell you any more now, but tonight . . . it has to be tonight." Then Barney hung up and rubbed his eyes.

"Marsh," he said, as if calling off a name on an invisible roster.

"That's a very annoying habit you have," Pace said.

Barney looked up. "What?"

"You always say a guy's name like you're reading the telephone book."

"Did you come in here to bug me, or do you have something to say?" Barney clicked the lucite ball against the glass top of his desk.

"Wait a second, wait a second," Pace said. "What's the matter with you, Barney? I've never seen you so . . . so distressed. And I understand. Believe me, I know what you've been through. He was a good man and *you* should be thankful for the opportunity of even *knowing* him."

Barney gave him a patronizing nod and crossed his legs as he twisted in his chair. He knew the paternal Pace was in the mood to talk, and now Barney wondered vaguely whether he had ever really liked him. It seemed as though Pace was only interested in Barney's personal life as a prelude to approaching a request for a business favor or new responsibility.

The thought had wound through his mind more than once. He remembered how Pace's anniversary gifts had been a hundred new shares of stock. Barney didn't realize exactly what it was about Marshall Pace. Somehow the cabled bond of association had stretched beyond ductility, and with exasperated shame, Barney wished he could throw Pace out of his office.

"Has it something to do with the I-Triple-E dropping your paper?" Pace asked.

Barney let the ball drop from his trembling fingers and watched it roll predictably across the desk and thud to the floor. "It's nothing to do with Bob *or* that silly convention," he blurted rudely. "What do you want, Marsh?"

Pace wouldn't let go. "See what I mean, Barney?" he said. "You've been in such a rotten mood lately."

Barney leapt up and kicked the ball beside his desk as he slapped at the air. "Goddamn it, Marsh. I've got a rotten job! People bugging hell out of me on the phone, and now you come in here and talk to me like I'm a goddamn sophomore again. Now, will you *please* tell me what you want to tell me and leave me alone?"

Pace, surprised, looked at Barney, and began nervously fondling his Navaho-hewn silver belt buckle. Barney thought it was corny.

"Look, Barney," he started in his paternal manner, "simmer down. I *did* come in with something important to say, but I just wonder if you're up to it." Pace's tone was an obviously placating one.

Barney sat back down and breathed heavily. "I'm sorry, Marsh. I appreciate your sympathy, but I'm just so goddamned nervous these days. I hate to be so touchy. I'm sorry."

"You've got to put those things aside now, Barney. Something's come up that's very important to Pace International, and we want you to help us."

"What is it?" Barney said, struggling for composure. He couldn't brush away the thought of his coming meeting with Charlie Blakemore.

"We've been talking about something that could change the entire course of our corporate objectives," Pace said. "In a nutshell, we're considering a merger with the DAWN Corporation."

"DAWN?" Barney exclaimed. "They haven't made a piece of hardware in their whole existence."

"Exactly," Pace said. "Nor have we ever undertaken a purely research investigation. It's a perfect marriage. But the important thing is that we want you, as P-I's research director, to codirect the new venture."

Barney seized the thought immediately and hugged it. DAWN! He didn't even know they were for sale, or would be amenable to any mergers, much less with an instrumentation firm. But what a chance! As co-director of a DAWN–P-I operation, he could talk some people into going for his antenna, his "giant ear" in the Nevada desert. Never mind the money, never mind the new prestige. He could at last get someone to finance his radio telescope, and finally let the world in on the verity of life outside the Earth.

Wait, Barney thought then. Hold on, Russom. You're *already* planning to let the world in on something. The bizarre plot wormed through the convolutions of his brain, and it was easy for him to let the brief thrill of the DAWN merger slip away. His thoughts vaulted in anticipation once again, turning lusty somersaults. His imagination raced in mental parabolas, defining and outlining, shading and coloring his image of the impossible plot.

He looked again at Pace and wondered how to word his evasion. "Look, Marsh," he said, "I can't right now. I *have* to have some time off."

"Fine," Pace interjected immediately. "This is still only in the talking stage, Barney. I was going to suggest a vacation anyway. Maybe right after the convention. I'd like you to be available and well rested by April."

"Yes, Marsh," Barney said. "I want to take Nancy to the lake for a while and get over this thing."

Barney looked at Pace blankly. He always felt uneasy when he lied, because he knew it showed.

He was not thinking of Pace International.

He was thinking of Norway.

Blakemore would have none of it.

For two hours, Barney paced around his den, not bothering to answer Charlie's brief interjections. The demons of obsession writhed across the papered walls of Barney's room like a horde of salamanders.

Now Blakemore tossed Barney's papers down. "Barney," he said, "this proves nothing. Absolutely nothing. All you talk about is theory. Absurd speculation."

"Now hold on and let me finish," Barney said impatiently. "Don't say anything. At least give me the opportunity to sum up the evidence."

"But you have no——"

"Now wait, Charlie! How do you think a rumor is born? If there was a rumor going around that you were going to leave your post at Sylmar and come to work at Pace International, why do you think it might have been started?"

"Well, people——"

"Hold on. It's completely untrue. You have never entertained such a thought. Understand? But yet someone would know that we were friends and had a common scientific interest. So from this premise it is not too hard to imagine that there might possibly be some basis for that rumor. Right?"

Charlie squinted at Barney. "But," he said, "the rumors would still be false."

"That's my point. But it's a better bet that it's true . . . true *rather* than being false."

Blakemore shook his head. "You would lose a fortune in Las Vegas, Barney. Only a fool would gamble a fortune on red simply because black has come up ten times in a row. Don't face gambler's ruin, Barney. Particularly on such a false premise. Your theory is absurd and, if I may say so, so are you."

Barney chuckled at his friend. "Wait a minute. You don't even know what I'm going to tell you yet, and you babble on about gambler's ruin. Now I'm going to go over here and have a drink. You don't drink. You don't smoke. Why? Because you think that God won't like it? Talk about absurdity! What's the formula for God's taste? You insist on putting everything in a test tube except your own beliefs. Do you want some Scotch or not?"

Charlie shook his head, irritably.

"Now hear me out!" Barney clinked the ice cubes into a glass and filled it with Scotch. He returned and sat across from Blakemore.

"The only *non*fact I have is the rumor about the humanoid corpses. Now, my clinical friend, here are the facts: Number one, there have been UFO sightings all over the entire world by reputable people and trained observers. Number two, the Air Force has consistently denied existence of UFO's and withheld any plausible explanation. Number three, at Wright-Patterson Air Force Base there is a division called FORTEC. It stands for Foreign Technology, Charlie. Don't you think it strange that Project Blue Book is part of FORTEC? Number four, my brother was in FORTEC, and he was a histopathologist. He is now dead, Charlie. I can't find one goddamn person to tell me what he was doing . . . how he died. Christ, I couldn't even see his *body!* Okay?"

Charlie sat back, finding himself listening. Looking

at his friend, he noticed a vein protruding on Barney's forehead. It crossed his mind that it was an effort for Barney even to take a breath.

"Shall I go on, Charlie?" Barney said.

"Go on."

"Number five," Barney said, shuffling quickly through the papers, pulling out an envelope. "In his last letter, or what was probably his last written word, my brother made mention of 'these things.' What things? What did he mean? He had a good salary. He had a nice wife, a new baby, and he was leaving the Air Force to teach at Stanford. Number six, you yourself expressed surprise at a pathology report from your friend Dr. Haggard in Norway. They claimed something my brother sent—which had to be some sort of tissue sample—didn't have a single carbon radical in it. Whatever it was, it was silicon-based. For Christ's sake, Charlie, a competent pathologist doesn't fool around with silly putty! Seven, there was a flight to Oslo and back to Wright-Patterson. Every member of that flight crew is now dead. And what's more, that flight occurred immediately after the crashing of the Spitzbergen Disc. Eight, each of those men were killed in an automobile accident on the same day. Can you write me an equation for that coincidence?"

Charlie interrupted. "All in all, Barney, I cannot bring myself to believe that the United States Air Force, or any portion of it, would resort to such malicious and underhanded activity. Further, I do not believe that a leading American scientist and rational human being could involve himself so personally in such inane conjecture. The Air Force, Barney, is on *our* side. They are under public scrutiny. I would be ashamed to think that our government would ever consider withholding such information, to say nothing of out and out murder."

"Public scrutiny?" Barney exclaimed. "How many people work for Blue Book? What's their budget? How many missiles do we have deployed in Turkey? When was the last time you ever heard of ball lightning?"

Charlie shrugged his shoulders. "That's not the point."

"Number nine," Barney ignored his friend. "You go home and examine your insurance policy. You will find, Charlie, that if you commit suicide, your beneficiary gets peanuts. My brother, so the holy Air Force says, killed himself. Yet they are giving his wife an unprecedented indemnity. I could go on all night. God knows, I've thought enough about it. It's driving me nuts. I've got to find out. They exist. They *have* to. There is no other explanation."

"Drink your Scotch, Barney," Charlie said, as Barney sat back at the point of exhaustion. Charlie was concerned over Barney's state of mind.

"I admit that the pathology report is highly extraordinary. I admit that Blue Book or FORTEC or whatever it's called has been strangely quiet on several celebrated phenomena. And as your friend, Barney, I will also concede that if all your facts are true, the existence of these corpses might be a logical conclusion. Granting you this, your scheme to get one and announce it to the world borders on lunacy."

Barney nodded. "Yes, I know. And you would think that a man in my position would write a letter to Washington, or ask some important mucky-muck for the classified information."

"Precisely," Charlie said. "They've locked men up for lesser schemes."

Barney sat back and smiled at Blakemore. "They won't lock *us* up, Charlie." ·

"Us!"

"You and me. Because we're going to get one. There is only one obstacle, and you know what that is."

Blakemore was afraid, fearful of what Barney was about to say.

Barney smiled as he spoke. "Who, Charlie, designed ELSIE?"

CHAPTER 9

Brigadier General Joe Quinting sat behind his desk and sipped coffee from a styrofoam cup as he read a story about how the Orioles expected to win the pennant this year. He looked up briefly to eye the round bottom of a young WAF brunette who dropped a sheaf of papers onto his desk.

His desk was gleaming neat, like a crystal prism. It was rimmed by a bank of black telephones. In the middle of the desk sat a single red telephone, which he hoped would never ring.

Before he finished his coffee, he was summoned over the intercom.

"Joe, come in here right away."

Quinting got up immediately, catching the young WAF before she left his office, and patted her smartly. "Cut it out," she said, as she had dozens of times before.

"It's only for good luck this time, sweetie. Teddyrook beckons again."

The girl eyed him and stuck out her tongue as he walked away.

"Teddyrook" was an affectionate name for Lieutenant General Theodore R. Castle, chief of military intelligence, domestic and foreign, who was responsible only to the Secretary of Defense. Teddyrook was short, squat, and hard, a chain smoker with pure white crewcut hair.

He was a legend, and the story still circulated from the lowest private right up through Joe Quinting himself, of the time in World War II when Teddyrook's B-25 crashed in North Africa behind German Panzer

69

division lines. Several weeks later, after being reported missing in action, Teddyrook thundered into Casablanca, stone drunk, missing a leg and driving a commandeered German munitions truck. He struggled on leg and cane into the temporary headquarters of Field Marshal Montgomery and flipped onto the commander's desk eight jingling dog tags of German officers.

Now Teddyrook had run out of room on his breast for more ribbons, and at 63 was the cleanup batter on the G-2 section softball team.

His stubby fingers thrust a decoded teletyped message on a legal-sized yellow sheet into Quinting's hand. "Read it," he said brusquely. "Sit over there, Joe."

Quinting looked at his commander and sat on the edge of a leather chair as he scanned the yellow paper.

4 MAR 68 XXX FR XXX ALADDIN XXX G710 XXX TO XXX COM G-2 CAMELOT FORTEC CASE 99—VSQURR—00700—ACTION REQ IMMEDIATE—FYI AND LANCER—XXX . . . CODE BGIN—766445—DECODE: O'NEILL—XXX . . . 000—SPTZ'BGN DISC MATERIAL CONFIRM PURE MAGNESIUM AND UNKNOWN ALLOY—DESTROYED NORWAY NO EVIDENCE.
XXX . . . 000—RPT ON ALIENS REVEALS TOTAL SIX REPEAT SIX—WRIGHT-PAT AFB FORTEC COMMAND CUSTODY. YYY . . . 000—NEW INFO MESSAGE FOLLOWS: DECODE: NORDHOFF—
YYY . . . NORWEGIAN COMMAND REFUSES AT THIS TIME TO RELEASE MORE INFO RE POWER ORIGIN ETC. OF DISC PEND. FURTHER INFO BY THEIR BOARD OF INQUIRY. SECOND REQUEST BY BRITISH GOVT. UNAUTHORIZED BY ALADDIN ALSO REFUSED. REQUEST PERMISSION TO CONTACT NORWEGIAN COMMAND RE MOSCOW INQUIRY. YYY . . . RUSSIAN CLAIM EVIDENCE OF SIGHTING

THROUGH LOCAL VILLAGERS AND IN-
TEND TO DEMAND THROUGH HUSH
CHANNEL PARTICIPATION IN FINDINGS.
REQUEST PERMISSION TO DECODE SO-
VIET THROUGH CHALLENGER.

YYY . . . ADD DEAD FILE—BROBS AND
TYLLENSEN AS OF YEST.

YYY . . . NEW TOTAL THOSE KNOWN
DOWN TO SEVEN REPEAT SEVEN IN-
CLUDING LANCER. LANCER OK RAISE TO
EIGHT SUGGEST BRIEF QUINTING.

YYY . . . NEW INFO MESSAGE FOLLOWS:
DECODE: MCCOY—

ZZZ . . . ORIGIN UNKNOWN BUT TURTLE
SUSPECTS EPSILON ETA FOR REASONS
OUTLINE IN FUTURE CORR. TURTLE
CONVINCED LUNAR LIAISON AS PRO-
JECTED BASE.

ZZZ . . . TURTLE REPORT TWO CASE 99
SIGHTINGS AREA FT. BECKENRIDGE
AND FT. HUACHUCA THIS DATE. OB-
SERVER FT. BRECKENRIDGE RELIABLE.
OBSERVER FT. HUACHUCA UNCON-
FIRMED.

ZZZ . . . NEW INFO MESSAGE FOLLOWS:
DECODE: ROSSI—

AAA. . . LANCER REQUEST URGENT AS
FOLLOWS NO DECODE: OENTO TIENS
WOENN EORIU OTIEK EHDLK THELT
TIENR DLUDE.

AAA . . . LANCER REQUEST URGENT AS
FOLLOWS NO DECODE: 97730 68887 30909
59708 69000 09488 00400 22551 41537.

Quinting looked at Castle in disbelief. "What's this?
An exercise?"

"Balls," Teddyrook snorted. "I'm going to tell you a
story that will curl that phony dyed hair of yours."

Quinting's smile evaporated quickly. Teddyrook
spent the next hour briefing him. When he was finished, Quinting was shocked but understood the ur-

gency and the desperate pains the government was taking to keep the secret.

He scanned the yellow code again. "What do those random additives at the end read?" he asked.

"It means pack your bags. We're leaving for Texas tonight to have chili beans with Lancer."

"And the coffin was even locked," Barney said as he and Charlie Blakemore were having dinner the next evening. "Do you believe that? It's really strange, Charlie. I'm telling you there's something—*something!* —behind it all. Can't I convince you that the biggest secret of this century is hidden at Wright-Patterson?"

Blakemore peered down into his soup and shook his head again. "Even if it *were* true, Barney, I couldn't break into that place. I realize I designed it, of course, but it's top secret. There are only a few people who even know how that system works."

"I know, I know," Barney said eagerly. "That's why you have to help me. If you can get us into that place where my brother worked, we'll have the evidence to break this thing wide open."

Charlie looked up pensively and allowed himself a faint smile. "It's an amusing thought, you know. Quite intriguing. Imagine having the opportunity of examining one of them." Charlie went back to his soup.

Barney quickly grabbed the opening. "That's exactly *it,* Charlie! Alien tissue. Other flesh. Can you guess what that would mean? Can you calculate the importance that would have on almost every area of human effort on this planet? And *we'd* be the ones who contributed all of it!"

Charlie looked up again. "I still can't believe the Air Force wouldn't make something like that public."

"Well," Barney said, "a military announcement like that would panic the world. That's what they're probably afraid of. But if we, as civilians and scientists, were to announce that we had examined one and found it *harmless,* the impact would be eased."

"But that would make the service look like fools and cowards. If they're protecting that building with one of our ELSIE's, a man would get shot down on the spot if he were caught."

Barney took his cup in both hands and leaned toward Charlie. "But don't you see? An announcement from us of alien life existing in the universe could very well lead to world peace! *Think* of it!"

"I suppose," Charlie said. "If we could only be sure."

He said "we," Barney thought. Maybe I've got him convinced. Then, aloud, he said, "How does ELSIE work, Charlie?"

Charlie smiled faintly again. "I'll tell you how it works, but I won't tell you how to crack it, Barney."

"Okay, okay. How does it work?"

"Well," Charlie started, and immediately assumed his professorial tone, "there are actually two systems: the inner zone and the outer zone. Both are set up on a bistatic radar basis. We have a system of posts, much like fence posts, along which are strung a line of conductors and sensors that generate a known electromagnetic field of specified frequencies. These—there are four, just like rails on a fence—are in tune, so that any time an unwanted material enters this field, an impedance is set up that changes the current along the line of sub-audio annunciators. This includes animals, snow, rain, and so forth, by the way. From the signal change, we can tell whether a crawling intruder or a flake of snow has generated the alarm."

Charlie beamed with pride as he spoke. "The whole fence line is mounted on a six-inch lime base, which reflects signals from about three feet on either side. So the intruder doesn't necessarily have to go directly between the lines—even if he only approaches the system, he'll be detected."

"Hell, that sounds simple. I could have guessed at that," said Barney.

"It is remarkably simple," Charlie went on, "but the major design problem was how to delicately balance these current-generating fields. If they're not balanced so that a current flows between them, then you have no security system. Also, by the way, you can have either an alarm or bell sound, or else arrange the signal so that the intruder doesn't know he's been detected."

"Would it be possible," Barney asked, "to dig *under* it?"

"Ha," Charlie said haughtily. "We're way ahead of you. You'd have to dig about twenty feet down. Don't you think if we were guarding a highly secret building or missile site that we'd have another line underground? Each transmitter—receiver pair, you know—provides up to twenty thousand cubic feet of coverage in volumetric installations."

Charlie sat back pridefully as Barney screwed his face into a concentrated grimace. "How about this," Barney said again. "Get to the supervisory control station, the annunciator, I guess, and knock that out."

Charlie shook his head. "It's *inside* the system."

"Like, what color was the monkey's house?"

"What?"

"I've always been interested in logic problems. We all know there is no such thing as a perfect security system. What's *your* flaw?"

Charlie just shook his head.

"It *can* be cracked, can't it?"

Charlie, caught up in his own pride, smiled again. "Yes, it can, and I suspect I'm the only one who could do it. I doubt if anyone else would know enough about its design to figure out how."

Barney drank his coffee in quick gulps. "I guess I'm at your mercy, Charlie."

"One thing, Barney. I'm still intrigued by all this—strictly as a theoretical exercise, of course—but how did you know one of our systems is guarding this place?"

Barney shrugged. "It's logical. You said yourself this type of system is for the highest security, *Case 99* places. And my brother was in one of the most secret places I know of. He couldn't even come home for dinner, for crissake. It *must* be an ELSIE."

"Well, I know it is, naturally. I know that all the security systems at Wright-Patterson are ELSIE's, in fact."

"And this FORTEC lab where my brother worked, if I'm right, should have one of its very own." He put down his cup and looked straight at Charlie. "Now, what do I have to do to convince you to help me, Charlie? I need you if I'm going to pull this scheme off."

Charlie hunched his shoulders. "Forget it. I think you're basing your whole argument on the fact that you couldn't see your brother. But they were probably right. They just don't have open caskets for suicides, I guess. Face it, Barney."

"You sound like that goddamned colonel at Wright-Patterson."

"I still say they could be right."

"And they could be wrong."

Charlie nodded.

"How would you like to face that gambler's ruin with me, Charlie?"

"What?"

"If I could prove to you that Bob isn't dead, would you go along with me?"

"You constantly amaze me. How could you prove that, Barney? *Write* to them?"

"Would you go with me then?"

"It's impossible to——"

"Dammit, Charlie. Would you or would you not go with me then?"

Charlie was quiet for several minutes as he pondered Barney's insistent question. He thought of his great pleasure at the roulette wheels, the outside chance that Barney could be right. The permutations and combinations couldn't be figured this time, though. All they had were variables and intangibles. Security systems and rumors.

"Let me put it this way," Barney pressed. "If my brother is not in that coffin, would you at least help me find him?"

Charlie looked at him. "Why, I suppose I would. But you still haven't told me how you can go about finding out with any degree of certainty."

Barney leaned closer to Charlie. He glanced over his

shoulder at the nearly empty restaurant, and lowered his voice as he spoke.

"Charlie," he said, "I'm willing to risk everything to find out what happened to Bob. I would disinter his coffin and break it open to find out if he is in there. And if that were in any way revealing, would you *then* follow through with me and kidnap one of the humanoids?"

Charlie folded his arms and suppressed his shock. He looked at his friend with an odd feeling, a mixture of fear and curiosity, blended with deep friendship and compassion for Barney. What disturbed him most, though, was his mounting interest, an almost sensual excitement. And he thought of the girl he never knew, the flavors of life he had never tasted, and the misty nights when he could speak only to the sea.

Trembling now, Charlie looked directly at Barney, and his glasses softly reflected the orange light from the candle. "Barney," he said quaveringly, "if your brother is not in that coffin, I'll help you break through ELSIE at Wright-Patterson."

CHAPTER 10

It was snowing when Barney and Charlie landed at South Dayton Airport. On the plane Barney had briefed Charlie on his plan to go to Carillon Park and climb over the corner wall of nearby Calvary Cemetery, close to the spot where Bob Russom was buried. Charlie was highly anxious throughout the trip, and Barney had been constantly reassuring him that the task was far easier than one would suspect.

Driving the rented car from the airport north on U.S. 25, Barney spoke with clinical detachment. "I only saw one guard when we were at the cemetery," he said. "All we have to do is climb over a small wall."

Barney caught himself. He was going to say "and start digging," but the words didn't come out. Charlie just nodded slowly.

"The earth will be soft," Barney resumed after a while, "even though the place is probably frozen over. There are two things in our favor, Charlie. First, they don't really bury these things six feet deep. The lid is probably only about two feet down. Secondly, it's highly unlikely they'll ever find out it was tampered with. It's a fresh grave, and the snow is on our side."

Charlie stiffened as Barney, in an antiseptic tone, rambled on. The realization pounced on his mind again. They were going to *dig up Barney's brother!* Good Lord, he thought, what are we doing here?

Barney was convinced the coffin would be empty. He wouldn't entertain the briefest thought that he might be wrong. After all, Barney was accustomed to being right.

Now his delirium was beginning to intensify. He clutched the plastic rim of the steering wheel tightly as he drove.

They swerved off the highway to Dixie Avenue and drove slowly past Carillon Park. "We'll leave the car there," Barney said. Charlie stayed quiet.

Passing the cemetery, Barney signaled in the direction of the entrance. "That's the only guarded place," he said. "They'll never hear us. We'll be about half a mile away, near the rear wall."

Charlie said nothing.

They patrolled by the cemetery once again, and then Barney drove to a hardware store to buy a pair of chain cutters—the heavy-duty kind, strong enough to snap a padlock. Before they reached a motel, he stopped several more times, each time recalling another item to buy—a stepladder, a flashlight, and two sturdy shovels. With each stop, Charlie's excitement rose, and outside the windshield wipers brushed clean the snow-fused glass.

By the time it was dark, the two men were sitting in their room, watching the chilly quiet of the winter night envelop the city.

Barney peered over the rim of the five-foot brick wall and found himself looking into the past. He was a robber Arab about to desecrate the sacred pyramidal tombs. He was about to strip away the secrets of a body carefully wrapped in pure linen and vaulted in a jeweled sarcophagus. He felt the cold wings of Horus, the falcon-god, brush his cheek, and he saw the ibis-headed Toth standing ready with a stylus to inscribe their names. And as he helped Charlie over, he saw Osiris, the god of the dead, standing on a distant pedestal watching the rape with silent, satisfied eyes.

They said nothing as they trudged through the darkness, and the gentle hush of the falling snow seemed to wrap them in an icy coat of apprehension. Charlie followed Barney closely as they stepped briskly to the grave site. The light from his flashlight blinked briefly, and Barney brushed the fresh snow from the flush-mounted plate that bore his brother's name. A quick wind whistled past their cold ears, and far off a dog barked.

Barney began shoveling, panting heavily and working much faster than the frail Blakemore. For twenty minutes they dug, piling the still-soft earth in a neat bank beside their work. With every shovelful, with every soft plop, the mound grew higher.

Suddenly Barney's shovel rasped the lid of the coffin, the sound seeming like an explosion in the bitter quiet. "Here it is," he murmured to himself, and he quickened his pace, clearing the lid of dirt. Charlie was wheezing, almost audible whimpers of both fatigue and nervousness. He dropped his shovel beside the grave before Barney had the lid cleared, and stood back, as if reneging on the vile plan.

Barney stepped into the shallow hole, and with gloved fingers took the chain cutter and attacked the hasp and lock with it. The clicking was familiar. Then, when the lock snapped, with each gasp and desperate finger-hold bringing them closer to their macabre treasure, Barney strained to open the lid. He stepped back. He heard Charlie exclaim loudly and he grappled in his coat for the flashlight again.

Straightening his arm, as if aiming a small pistol, Barney snapped on the beam, and the thin thread of light flashed quiet white streaks as the snow slashed across its path.

Charlie rushed quietly to stand beside Barney, and they both peered down, following the light to its target.

"Oh, my God," Charlie gasped. "Oh Lord, Barney."

Barney gazed down and said nothing. His mind buckled at the image carried to it by revolted eyes.

Barney dropped to his knees and the flashlight flipped into a pile of snow. He began weeping mutely, and Charlie seized his head in his arms, as he would a crying child. Barney wept hard, racking sobs, and Charlie nestled him in pity.

It was a while before Charlie could get Barney to regain his composure and cover the grave.

For there, in the faint and gauzy light of the snow-swept flashlight beam, was the decaying body of a young Negro airman.

CHAPTER 11

The trim Air Force jet cut through the light fog of Washington and banked southward. Aboard the finely appointed plane, Teddyrook and Joe Quinting loosened their ties and lounged on bright chrome and leather chairs with a bottle of gin. The two were the only men in the main cabin. Teddyrook still had a small briefcase locked to his wrist. Quinting took a snub-nosed .38 from his waist and set it beside him.

"That's going to break one of my ribs, someday," he said.

"Why don't you find a smaller one," Teddyrook asked, sipping his drink.

Quinting just shrugged. He reached across a small walnut table between them and added another ice cube to his glass. Then he glanced out the window at the clear sky.

"Can you tell me what this is all about, now?"

Teddyrook knocked on the briefcase on his lap. "You know almost all of it already," he said to Quinting. "Got a few more dead from Wright-Patterson and some guy thinks he knows where that disc was from. The big thing, actually, is the Russkies."

"What'd *they* do?"

"They got wind of what's going on and they want in on it. They grilled a few Norwegian fishermen or something and got the whole story. Now they're demanding they be sent at least two of the things and a piece of the disc. Naturally, Lancer is going to tell them to go screw. The only thing is that we don't want them mouthing off about the whole deal." He took another drink.

"Seems to me," Quinting said, "that we'd gladly give them something to keep them quiet. Won't they get a little pissed off?"

"Sure they will, but they're scared as hell, same as us. Only we got the goods and they don't, so we figure they'll stay in line at least for a while, until we get some more info on these things. And second, they've already got themselves a beautiful reputation for announcements like that. They invented the airplane, spaghetti, and baseball, remember? What'll everyone think if they suddenly come out and say they have six bodies from outer space?"

"Still sounds like a gamble to me."

"Well, it *is,* but that's why we're going to Texas tonight. If Lancer or Challenger tries to wheel and deal with them, every newsman in the world will smell something going on. Now they want me to go to Moscow and negotiate it with them. You'll run the shop when I leave, but it probably won't be for a week or so."

"Hell, what's to negotiate? Screw 'em. Why do we have to massage them?"

"That's what I think, too, but Lancer apparently has some different ideas. One of our agents there thinks we can get something good from them in return. Like more pressure on the Chinks or something. I'll kind of shoot through the hush channel mostly, I guess. Still not sure exactly what it is they expect me to do. Old Alexei doesn't trust a uniform, you know."

"But why am *I* along?" Quinting asked.

"We want you in on it from the start just in case they get me or something serious happens to snag us in Russia. But don't get too excited, yet. We'll probably have one bourbon and branchwater tonight and spend the rest of the time talking about the Pedernales."

Lake Tahoe straddles the California and Nevada line. Ponderosa pines and Douglas firs ring its perimeter. On the east side, however, the area has been victimized by the ugly exploitation of the Nevada gambling interests. Here, high-rise casinos lure and suck dollar after dollar from greedy people with feeble hopes. Blaring neon invitations promise fun and excitement, high-priced entertainment, the thrill of something for nothing.

Off California Highway 50, just south of the lake, Barney and Nancy owned a cabin on the south fork of the American River. The cabin itself was ideal for the purpose. Its slanted roof gave a view of the rushing river and yet prevented anyone from prying in. It was equipped with a small kitchen, a large family room, a den, and two bedrooms. Each room had a picture window that afforded a spectacular view of the high Sierras. The cabin sat on a relatively flat area a hundred yards from the river. One had to park well away from the cabin and pack in to reach it.

By the time Charlie and Barney returned from Dayton and reached the cabin site, Barney still had not recovered from the shocking experience. His actions had grown quick and staccato, like those of a frightened sparrow. Charlie, on the other hand, had become analytical in his approach, and now looked forward with scientific zeal to the grotesque plot.

Charlie had brought some supplies with him, and began to set up a small lab. His fingers trembled as he unpacked the beakers and vials and, at one point, a few slides tumbled to the floor—pushed by anticipatory haste. He whistled lowly as he worked, clinking and tinkling in a far corner of the paneled den. He was thinking only of detailing a chemical study of the stilled victims of their kidnap scheme, while Barney sat at a small desk in a straight-backed chair, doodling and sketching on pieces of paper. Barney was perspiring in the heated room.

Charlie watched his friend vacillate between irrational frenzy and cool calculation. Barney seemed possessed by two simultaneous devils, he thought—one the inquisitive zealot, one a courier of madness. Barney's eyes would grow turgid one minute, as he dwelt upon a particular idea, and the next instant he would seem virtually melancholy. He was like a manic-depressive who knows and understands his affliction but enjoys the traumatic switch from man to machine and back.

"Let me tell you how we can get through," Charlie said, and his familiar mannerisms took over as he lectured. "It's like creating a hole, but filling it at the same time. A good analogy would be drilling a hole in a piece of thick wood. You're creating the hole, but filling it with the drill bit at the same time. In other words, there would still be some matter along a straight line through the hole, even though it would be steel instead of wood."

Barney nodded. "Okay, okay," he said impatiently.

"So what we will do is this," Charlie went on. "I think I can make a small device that could generate its own magnetic field. It would have very small circuits and some solid-state amplifiers to step it up. We'll be able to generate whatever current we want around our bodies.

"What we have to do, though, is determine exactly what we'll be wearing the night we—er, go in. Right down to the very fillings in our teeth, Barney. We'll have to weigh ourselves very carefully immediately before we go to Wright-Patterson. This is because we have to determine our exact mass, and precisely how our bodies, clothes and all, will disrupt the energy field. Then we will tune my little device, and turn it on when we approach the fence. In this way—rather ingenious, if I say so myself—we can pass through the system while maintaining the same current that existed without us. We will, in effect, become like the drill bit passing through the wood, except we will not be metallic."

"How big would it be?"

"It might be a copper mesh belt which would encase our generators. They'd radiate electromagnetic energy around us in a cycloid pattern, so that we'd in essence transmit and distribute the power equally. One thing, though, Barney."

Barney looked up.

"We still could get caught."

"Even with us transmitting the proper frequency?"

Charlie nodded. "They *change* frequencies throughout the system at random intervals, just to guard against some scheme similar to mine. If we are within the field at the time they change, we'll set off the alarm or——"

"Or what?"

"Or be electrocuted. We'll only be in there for a few seconds, but that would be all it takes if they shift while we're in it."

"How often do they change frequencies?"

Charlie just shrugged. "That's a secret I can't know. Maybe every five minutes, maybe every hour. One other thing."

"What now," Barney sighed.

"Have you thought about dogs?"

"Dogs?"

"Sentry dogs. Police dogs. There's a chance they, too, will be deployed there."

"Hell," Barney said. "If your system is so all-fired goddamn good, why would they have dogs?"

"Just a thought. It's probably unlikely in a populated base, but——"

"Maybe we should take a gun," Barney said.

Charlie shook his head. "No. Such a large piece of metal would be too conductive for my tiny system. We'll even have to take the buckles off our belts and the eyelets out of our shoes."

Barney stood up suddenly and snapped his fingers. "Charlie, you're really convinced, now, aren't you? Now that we *know* they didn't bury him. He may not be dead—maybe they've got him locked up."

Charlie smiled faintly. "I'll never forget what we saw in that coffin. Never."

"Wait 'til we get inside that goddamn building."

For the next two hours the two men planned their movements in detail. Outside a wind came up, rustling the needles of the pine trees and flicking softly at the shutters. A coyote howled somewhere, and a late-returning woodpecker sought hungrily for bugs in a tree.

They speculated on how many persons would know

about such beings in existence. Charlie recalled the famous Manhattan Project, which during World War II was probably the biggest secret the world had known. But there had been more than a hundred people in on it, and security hadn't been breached. How many could keep such a secret today? Barney guessed less than a dozen. The President, he said, and probably the Secretaries of Defense and State. Probably two or three high-ranking military men, maybe a few FBI or CIA people. Who else? To keep the secret, someone had killed the flight crew, and perhaps Barney's brother. Was it possible he had completed whatever research he was doing, and now they simply had no more use for him? Did they also kill whoever knew about the project in Norway? That would be something else again. Certainly the disc crashed on their territory, apparently over the Svalbard Islands in the Norwegian Sea. It was also certain a lot of fishing activity took place in that area, so what is the Norwegian government doing to keep the locals quiet? What about the Soviets? Would they be in on it, since Norway's a neutral country?

What about the creatures themselves? Are they intact? Are they, in fact, all dead? Was that actually a tissue sample that Bob had sent to Oslo, leading the professor there to mistake the silicon-based sample for a toy object? If they are silicon-skinned, would they be stored in formaldehyde? Charlie suggested not, probably they'd be encapsulated in some other solution. The two men could only surmise, from these and other thoughts, that the beings were movable.

But what was the ultimate fate of the FORTEC project? When would they announce the existence of the beings? Would they announce it at all, fearing public panic and world chaos? And how do these creatures treat their own dead?

Could they themselves right now be plotting the very same conspiracy, to transport their dead back to whatever strange planet harbored them?

Barney had drawn up a timetable. Right after the

convention in New York, they would attend a two-day symposium scheduled at Wright-Patterson on Flight Instrumentation and Fire Control. Each of them had a legitimate interest in it, through their respective work, and they agreed that wangling an invitation wouldn't be difficult. After the symposium, during which they would be put up at the base VOQ, they would steal into the lab. Would there be a guard? They didn't know.

Barney asked Charlie, "Can we get the body back out through the system without being detected?"

"No," Charlie said, his face dropping. "We simply can't calculate the mass until we see and weigh it. We'd be discovered when we went back through the ELSIE."

Barney smiled. "If we went back *through* it."

"What do you mean? We'd *have* to go back through it."

"Remember what you said at dinner? The control for the security fence is *inside* the system. When we get in, couldn't we get to the control box and simply deactivate it?"

Charlie's eyes lighted up. "I don't see why not. I have to be very careful, but I could take a look at the schematics of the system, to be sure. It just might be possible. Everything is probably controlled by the central station."

Charlie thought a minute. "You know, we once had a skunk loose in our plant and two men showed up to search it out and take it away. They were from some exterminator firm. Well, it turned out that they had let the skunk loose themselves the night before and were actually industrial spies taking secrets out of Sylmar Electronics. They were so nervy and had such an outlandish scheme, it almost worked."

"Right," Barney said. "But ours *will* work."

Charlie shook his head. "I can't believe we're actually going through with this."

Barney's eyes were wide again as he savored the plot. "I have off from P-I until after the convention, so I'll have time to help you fix the equipment. We'll meet at the convention and act as if we're just meeting professionally. Then we'll go to Wright-Patterson together."

Charlie nodded and fell silent. Barney drummed his fingers on the table and Charlie nervously fiddled with his thick spectacles. He felt a quick tightness clutch his chest, and the nagging impossibility of it all confronted him once again. But he, too, felt a strange alliance with Barney. He now shared Barney's conviction. He was willing to pay a costly price for the opportunity of his scientific life. The challenge was presented, and the bait was consumed. "Barney," he said finally.

Barney looked up from his sketches.

"What if they catch us before we can come back here and make the announcement?"

"Probably arrest us, at the very least. But they would keep it quiet, and persons of our position would have a good chance of begging off. There really isn't much they could do."

"The *they* I was referring to, Barney," Charlie said, "was not the United States Air Force."

CHAPTER 12

"If you pinch me one more time, I'm going to kick you right where it hurts!" The pretty WAF had turned around to face Joe Quinting as he got up and walked toward the door of his office.

"It *already* hurts, baby. Just for more good luck, that's all. Teddyrook has summoned me again."

"Just stay away from me."

Quinting smiled and strode briskly out the door and down the hallway.

In Teddyrook's office, Quinting took out a panatella and, without lighting it, stuck it between his teeth and sat on the couch.

The General was grim. Joe noticed a yellow tele-typed sheet on the desk in front of him.

Teddyrook looked up, frowning. "You don't know anything about graves at Wright-Patterson, do you?" It was a statement more than a question.

Quinting was surprised. He looked blankly at Teddy-rook.

The General waved the yellow sheet at Quinting. "You're not going to like this, Joe. There's something else we haven't told you."

Quinting read:

19 MAR 68 XX FR XXX ALADDIN XXX G710 XXX TO XXX COM G-2 CAMELOT FORTEC CASE 99—VSQRR—08800—AC-TION REQ IMMEDIATE—FYI AND LANC-ER—XXX . . . CODE BGIN—766485—DE-CODE: NORDHOFF—BBB . . . 000—

WRIGHT-PAT GRAVE TAMPERED WITH RE SECURITY BREACH.
BBB . . . 000—LOCK CUT. COFFIN OPENED. URGENT DISCOVER CULPRIT RE COVER STORY OF RUSSOM BURIAL SITE. REPEAT URGENT. SUSPECT SUCH AGENT NOW KNOWS SOMETHING OF CAMELOT FORTEC.
BBB . . . 000—ALSO SUSPECT SOVIET CONNECTION. PROCEED WITH MOSCOW PLAN IMMEDIATE HASTE. ASSIGN QUINTING IMMEDIATE.
BBB . . . 000—NEW FORTEC PATHOLO-GIST MAJ. WALTER W. WORTHINGTON. AO 465867739. REC FOLLOWS.
CCC . . . 000—NEW MESSAGE FOLLOWS. URGENT. NO DECODE. FYI ONLY.
CCC . . . DLRKR SLEIT TOWOS ZPEKT SPVMT SPELR TOEKT CCC . . . OOO— NEW MESSAGE FOLLOWS. URGENT. NO DECODE. FYI ONLY.
CCC . . . 38465 20485 48601 11495 40612 90464 30586

"Look, Teddy," Quinting said, "I still don't know what the hell you're talking about. You always clammed up on me, goddamn it, whenever I asked about Bob Russom. Now for crissakes, what's this about his grave?"

The red-faced general slammed his fist on his desk. "Tell me everything you know about him."

Quinting's anger began to rise. He sighed heavily and glared across the room. "Not much, except that his brother's my best friend. Good scientist, nice guy, all that sort of thing. Suicide a couple of weeks ago. I assume he couldn't take the FORTEC jazz."

The general's tone grew hard. "Joe," he said evenly, "it wasn't suicide."

Quinting looked at him and didn't move. He bit hard on his cigar.

Teddyrook got up and began pacing in front of the large window. "Look," he began. "This is the rest. He was the guy examining these things and he caught some disease from them and kicked off in the lab. Naturally, we couldn't tell his family about it, so we planted the suicide bit with Colonel Rubin at Wright-Pat. And some corpsman accidentally got a look-see inside FORTEC. We put him in the hole to make it as real as possible. He had no family and all that crap."

Quinting was shocked. "Jesus," he said. "How the hell could——"

"We had no choice, Joe. We couldn't remove the Russom guy for fear of contamination. Apparently we *still* don't know exactly what the hell to do with the whole mess. This new guy, Worthington, will probably get it too. But we have to learn *more* about those god-damn things!"

Quinting slapped his knees and stood up. He walked to the center of the room and glared at Teddyrook. His voice rose. "And you didn't tell me about it because you thought I'd crack up or something? Because I knew *Barney* so well?"

The older man stopped his pacing. He faced Joe, ignoring Quinting's angry tone. He welcomed arguments, but this time he didn't flare back. He shrugged instead.

"Yeah," Teddyrook said. "That's exactly it. And I'm sorry."

Quinting stepped up to him and gestured to his own shoulders. "Listen, Teddy, I didn't get these goddamn stars for running a kind hearts society. Christ, I've killed guys from five miles over Saipan to a stinking Paris sewer. God *damn* it, Teddy!"

Teddyrook's eyebrows lifted. He was surprised at Joe's outburst.

"Dead's dead, I know that! I'm no Holy Ghost who breathes new life into the poor bastards! *I've* been around the block a few times." Quinting spun again and walked off, talking now to the wall. "Now, is there anything *else* I should know? Do I now know *everything?*"

"Everything," Teddyrook said. "And again, I'm

sorry. I screwed up, I guess, but it's not all that serious. I only thought it wasn't important at the time, and there was no sense bugging you emotionally after that weird briefing I gave you."

"Well, let's forget it," Quinting said. "The important thing now is what the hell do we do about it?"

"That's where you come in," Teddyrook said, going back to his desk. "I'm flying to Moscow tonight. You are now in charge of the whole shmear. Find out who the hell eyeballed the grave as soon as you can. It's my guess it's some Russky working for Rubin."

"What about Major Peterson over in armament?"

"Nah," Teddyrook said. "We've been watching him closely for a long while and he hasn't sent out anything important for a month or so. He wouldn't pull something like this off anyway. Too stupid."

Quinting ticked off more names of double-agent officers at Wright-Patterson in his mind, but dismissed them all. Teddyrook was right. It had to be either someone brand new or a civilian.

Civilian.

Joe Quinting tried not to change expression as he pondered the awful possibility. He recalled the information he had given Barney, which amounted to an alarming security breach, but there was nothing to do about it now. The fact was, he realized with guilt, that the information was out and now someone else knew about the phony burial. Could Barney have done it? The thought haunted him. He wouldn't tell Teddyrook, but Quinting had a strong and steadily convincing notion that the grave robber was *not* a Soviet agent.

"Colonel Rubin's investigating officer will have a report for you first thing in the morning," Teddyrook was saying. "When you get it, start tracking the bastard down. This is highly critical, Joe. You're the only other G-2 in on this whole cruddy mess. When I come back from Moscow, I want it over with. No delays. No stalling. Get on it as soon as you leave this office."

Teddyrook went over to the desk and took up the

yellow sheet again. "Now I'll decode this last part for you: Don't confine him, don't lock him up." He looked coldly over at Quinting and his lips remained stiff as he breathed the order.

"I don't care *who* he is, or how high-ranking," Teddy-rook said. "Even if you find out it was *me,* for crissakes." He took another breath. "When you find the bastard, *kill him.*"

CHAPTER 13

Ginger Russom was feeding her daughter in the kitchen of Barney's house. Nancy was briskly stirring an iron pot filled with her special minestrone soup. Barney would have time for a bowl before Monty Kuehner would come by to take him to San Francisco International Airport.

Nancy walked into the bedroom where Barney was hastily packing his two suitcases, cramming the clothes roughly into the bags. She approached him from behind quietly and quickly grabbed his shoulders, kissing the back of his head.

Barney jumped. "Don't," he exclaimed.

Nancy laughed. "Can't I kiss my own husband? Sorry, I didn't mean to scare you."

In mock gesture Barney pounded his heart with his fist. "You just gave me heart failure. It wasn't the kiss, believe me."

Nancy pointed to a large black satchel in the corner. "What's *that* suitcase for? Where did you get it?"

Barney glanced at the satchel. "Oh," he said, "it's just some gear from the plant that I'm taking with me to the show. I didn't want to trust the shippers with it."

"Soup's ready. Come into the kitchen and grace us with the pleasure of your company. We haven't seen much of you lately with that big deal you're working on. And besides, your niece gained three pounds and you haven't had time to notice."

Barney wrapped his arm around her shoulders and walked into the kitchen.

"When are you coming back?" Nancy asked.

Barney sat down before the steaming bowl. "Right

after the convention," he said without hesitation. "So you girls be sure to get back from the cabin by then. Incidentally, don't disturb the stuff I let Charlie Blakemore set up in the rear bedroom. I'm going to let him study his bugs there for a week after the show."

"Oh," Nancy replied, "we'll be back when you get home."

Barney was imperceptibly relieved. Now there would be no one at the cabin when he and Charlie returned with their extraordinary loot.

Barney slurped the last drop of soup and took the little girl on his knee. "She's a real little swinger, isn't she?"

Ginger beamed.

"I don't see any three new pounds. *Feels* like at least five, though."

The girl grasped Barney's two middle fingers and began bouncing. "Hey," he asked, "what's this red between her fingers?"

"The doctor said it was just a mild eczema. I've been putting some salve on it, but it doesn't seem to be going away. She's due to see the doctor next week if it isn't better by then. Babies get these little skin disturbances. It's normal."

"How *do* babies get rashes, anyway?"

"I think she probably picked it up from Bob," Ginger said.

"From Bob?" Barney thought of his dead brother and the hideous secret he had uncovered.

"Yes," Ginger continued. "Bob had some sort of skin irritation on his hands. It seemed to be getting worse, but he wouldn't do anything about it. Just kept working. The last time," Ginger's voice began to crack, "I mean when he went to work the last time, his hands were covered with it."

Barney's curiosity was alerted, but he did not pursue it further, and was thankful when Turp barked from the front porch, announcing the arrival of Monty Kuehner.

Conventioneers from Pace International were staying at the Essex House on Central Park South. The hotel was convenient to the Coliseum—a five-minute walk. There was an air of frivolity among the New York visitors. Some had spent more time than usual in the Essex House lounge, others were frantically making telephone calls to their plants, checking on delayed equipment and last-minute price changes. Barney registered as quickly as possible, insisting that he alone carry the new black satchel. In his room he changed into a fresh shirt and decided to visit the lounge and go to bed early.

The lounge was buzzing with preconvention excitement. As he walked in, he knew he would probably be stuck with the tab for the entire mob of P-I employees. Dave Scott, P-I's publicity director, spotted him immediately and gestured for Barney to join him. Scott had been drinking all afternoon, and when he was high, he spoke more loudly than usual.

This, too, grated on Barney.

Barney ordered a Scotch-over and sat down next to Dave. "You're coming to the hospitality suite, aren't you, Barney?" Dave asked.

"Oh, Christ, not that again. I'd forgotten about it. Hospitality suites are a goddamn waste of the corporation's money."

"But necessary for us flacks and salesmen. Besides, I've got some press guys coming who want to see you."

"Okay, okay. I'll try to make it. What room is it?"

"Suite 1401," Dave said. Barney nodded.

Suddenly Dave looked up. "Hey, check who just walked in."

Barney looked over his shoulder and saw Carl Phillips, the *Aviation and Space Management* editor who had written the article on ball lightning as an explanation for UFO sightings. Barney grimaced when he saw him and turned back to Dave. "That son-of-a-bitch," he said.

Dave laughed. "Hold on, he's not so bad. He's a little fruity, I think, but he's done P-I a helluva lot of good."

"He's an idiot," Barney said defiantly.

"Well, the idiot just noticed us and is walking over to the table."

Barney sighed heavily as he anticipated Phillips' presence.

Phillips was nattily attired in a porkpie hat, the parti-colored feather of which matched the man's reputation. He wore a yellow shirt and a red paisley tie, which was complemented by a blossoming paisley handkerchief.

Barney glanced at the pointy-toed shoes coming his way.

"Well, well," Phillips said, seating himself without invitation. "The guest of honor and his mouthpiece."

"The man from the Pistachio Palace," Barney said acrimoniously. "How many other nuts did they let out this evening?"

Phillips ignored the jab, and Scott hastily ordered himself another tranquilizing martini.

"Dave," Phillips said, still ignoring Barney, "a guy named Kuehner is giving a paper Thursday afternoon on a new application of one of your analog-integrated circuits. I'd like the details now on that one."

Dave said, "Yeah, we're having a press conference right after that session to talk more about it to you guys."

"That's not what I asked you," Phillips said haughtily. "I'd like it tonight so I can have my story prepared."

Dave shrugged at him. "Can't do it, Carl. It's secret until then. You know how they are about the originality of their technical sessions."

Phillips started to interrupt again and press for more, but Barney slammed his fist down on the table, inches from Phillips' slender hand.

"God damn it, Phillips," he roared. "You *can't* have it. You can't have shit from us, as far as I'm concerned."

Phillips was unperturbed. "Here now, we don't have to shout, do we?"

Barney said nothing.

Phillips went on. "Are you still mad about my article on ball lightning?"

"You're damn right I am," Barney said. "It was stupid, erroneous, and obviously an Air Force plant."

Phillips smirked at him. "A lot of our readers found it interesting. As I'm sure they will the special seminar on hot carrier diodes tomorrow. Do you plan to attend?"

Barney glared at him icily. "Look, Phillips. What you guys are doing is wrong and you know it. You guys are so profit-motivated, you'll do most anything to increase your advertising revenue. Even sensationalizing like a sex-crazed tabloid."

"Please," Phillips said in sarcastic mockery. "You're speaking of the bible of the industry."

"Are you serious?" Barney said sternly. "What kind of bible publicizes and openly advocates a war that kills babies and old women, just so you can sell a few more copies of your rag to other people who make their living at killing?"

"Including Pace International, of course."

Scott moaned.

"We're making out very well, thank you, without building weapons."

"I wish you wouldn't talk of sensationalism, Mr. Russom," Phillips said. The term mister was again abrasive on Barney's mind; it was said with full knowledge of his deserved title. "After all, I think I did a great service to the industry and to the convention by helping to knock your imaginative seminar on UFO's off the agenda."

Barney stood up abruptly and threw the remainder of his drink into Phillips' face. Scott also leaped to his feet in reaction, murmuring an obscenity as he did so. Phillips merely smirked, and blinked through the veil of cold fluid. He slowly wiped his face with his paisley kerchief, as Barney stormed from the room amid the rising hum of surprised onlookers.

Barney called Room Service, remembering the last time he had done so, and ordered dinner sent up. Then he turned on the television set and saw the same skinny man with a moustache delivering the evening's weather report. He sat down and poured himself a drink from the bottle he'd brought with him.

After dinner, he kicked off his shoes and watched a movie, during which he fell asleep in the soft chair. At two o'clock in the morning, his telephone rang, waking him. The first he saw was the hissing snow of the blank TV screen, and he stumbled sleepily to the phone.

"Barney?" the voice said, a distantly familiar voice which was camouflaged by Barney's stupor.

"Yes?" he said, still shaking off the sleep. The party on the other end hung up the receiver.

Puzzled, Barney realized he was still dressed and began peeling off his clothes. Who could *that* have been? His mouth felt cottony, and he went in to brush his teeth. A knock at the door once again disturbed him.

"Surprise, surprise, pal." General Joe Quinting flashed his bright, toothy smile at Barney from under his deep tan. Joe Quinting was in his uniform.

"Joe!" Barney shouted at him and beckoned him in as he reached for a robe on the bed. "What the hell are *you* doing here?"

Quinting flipped his ashes on the floor and smiled again. "Got a razzle-dazzle job, pal. We ace airmen and high-ranking officials get all around the country, you know. Got any booze?"

Barney laughed, glad to see his old friend. "That you who called a minute ago? I didn't recognize your voice." He pointed to the bottle on the dresser.

"I just wanted to be sure I wouldn't be walking in on some teeny-boppers on their honeymoon."

Barney gave him a drink and Quinting sat down, throwing his cap onto the bed.

"Seriously, why are you here? Going to the show?"

"Nah, tell you about it later. First of all, how's Nancy?"

"Fine," Barney said, pouring himself a drink. "She's at the lake this week with Ginger and my niece."

"How's she getting along?"

"Great. Everything's fine," Barney said, but thought briefly of the red rash on the baby's fingers. "And Maggie?"

"Peachy. Don't like to be away from her so much. I'm thinking of getting out of this rotten war racket anyway. Some of the shit they're giving me now is a little too much."

"Like what?" Barney asked.

"Like now, pal. Yeah, I'm here for a reason. I've got to tell you some disconcerting news and ask you an embarrassing question."

The last shred of sleep slipped from Barney's mind and a gulp of Scotch braced him again. Quinting couldn't know, he thought, he couldn't possibly know.

"What's up, Joe?" Barney forced a casual tone.

"First of all, and you can take a poke at me when I'm through, but I have to tell you the background. You know those names I gave you?"

"Oh, that," Barney chuckled. "I was really loony then."

Quinting pressed, "What did you do with those names?"

Barney looked at his friend. "Nothing. I was nutty. I think I even lost the list."

Quinting was relieved for an instant. "Well, it seems somebody has tampered with your brother's grave and —I hesitate to say this, Barney—but I have direct orders to get a statement from you."

"Are you kidding?"

Joe shook his head. "No," he said evenly. "Some nut has been messing around the cemetery."

Barney began to be afraid, and worried about the credibility of his feigned indignance. "Statement! My statement is that I'm appalled. What do you mean, *tampered*? Who would tamper?"

"Well, I know you were pretty mad about that closed coffin and you really made a big thing out of it."

"Joe," Barney blurted. "What do you mean, *tampered*?"

"Well, the covering earth was disturbed."

"Disturbed or was it dug up?"

Joe reluctantly nodded. "Yeah, Barney. It was dug up, and the casket broken into."

Barney was on his feet. "And you think *I* did it?"

"No, no, *I* don't. I just have orders to ask."

"Well, listen, Joe. I have not been back to that cemetery since the burial, and I don't intend to go back for the rest of my life, even though I'll be at Wright-Patterson after this convention for a symposium. I have a good notion to demand a full investigation from that Colonel Rubin. God *damn* it, Joe."

Joe looked at his friend. "Please, Barney, let me handle it. Listen, I'm going to find out. I won't know any more until I get the report from the investigating officer next week."

"Did they do anything with Bob?" Barney asked.

"I don't know." Joe Quinting lied to his friend. "I'll have to wait."

CHAPTER 14

When Barney awoke the next morning he wasn't hungry, so he skipped breakfast and decided to walk to the Coliseum rather than take a cab. The brisk New York air revived him immediately, as horns honked beside him and the Gotham hordes were overpowered for the moment by thousands of visiting engineers.

A friend joined him on the walk as he strode across the first intersection. He reminded Barney of the preceding evening's episode in the lounge as he talked mirthfully of how the story had spread throughout the evening's round of welcoming parties and barhopping groups. Barney merely grunted.

At the convention and exhibit, he went directly to the morning's special session on hot carrier diodes in Room D. He saw Charlie Blakemore sitting alone in a rear row, perusing his program. The room was only half full, and it gave Barney a faint satisfaction. He was certain his own seminar would have packed the hall.

Charlie looked up as Barney sat next to him, and his face was tense. "Morning," Barney said. Charlie nodded, waiting for Barney to say more.

Barney didn't. Charlie then looked up at him and said, "You'd do well to try not to draw too much attention to yourself. Isn't that what you told me to guard against?"

"What do you mean?"

"What is this about your throwing a drink in somebody's face?"

"He deserved it. The place isn't very full, is it?"

Charlie scanned the audience. "The first sessions

103

usually aren't. I didn't think there would be much interest in the subject, anyway."

Barney smiled. "I could have told them that. All they do is bitch about not having any unique technical sessions, yet they insist on subjects like this. Christ, every goddamn engineer in the country knows about hot carrier diodes. And if he doesn't, he just doesn't care."

"You're probably right," Charlie said. "Did you get the tools in okay?"

Barney nodded. "Brought them in a small satchel."

Charlie glanced around again. A fat man with dark glasses looked at him from across the aisle, and two crew-cut young engineers from Texas waved at him from the front row. On the podium five men were bustling for seats, and one of them held a sheaf of papers and tried to act pleasant.

The lights dimmed a bit and the audience quieted as the chairman blew roughly into the open microphone. Then acoustical feedback whined shrilly through everyone's ears, forcing gritted teeth and not a little physical pain. Barney once again chuckled silently at the fact that here were seventy-five thousand electronics engineers, and still this feedback reverberated through every symposium hall in the huge auditorium.

"I'm getting out of here," Barney said. "I just wanted to tell you all the stuff is in my room and I've made the arrangements for us to attend the Wright-Patterson symposium. They'll have our badges and clearance at the gate. A Colonel Roffelson will meet us and check us into the VOQ. I suggested a tour of the base, too, and he thought it could be arranged. Might come in handy."

Charlie nodded again nervously. "What night are we going to do it?" In his voice echoed the excited hush of the schoolboy stealing a lunchbox in the cloak room.

"We leave for Dayton Wednesday night. I've reserved a station wagon at the airport." The thought of transporting such strange cargo in as mundane a carrier as a station wagon surged through Charlie. "We'll go directly to the VOQ and attend the first session Thursday. Hopefully we'll have a chance to reconnoiter the FORTEC installation. If things go right, Charlie, we can make the attempt Friday night after the closing cocktail party. Everyone will be going home that evening, but I've told them we'll be tired after this whole week and we'd like to stay over and leave early Saturday morning. That way we can drive right to the airport, maybe before sunrise, and be off before the base is alerted. They've even helped us get reservations out of Dayton early Saturday." Barney paused and looked at Charlie. "Of course, we won't be needing them."

"What about flying out to Tahoe?"

"I've made arrangements with a private pilot in Athens, near Dayton."

The speaker on the stage was droning on about current reversal and power capabilities. Everyone seemed mesmerized and sleepy, and one man on the seminar was shaking his head slowly in disagreement with the speaker. The place resembled a wake where each had a chance to deliver his own version of a eulogy.

Charlie tugged at Barney's sleeve as Barney started to rise. "Why don't we have dinner together tonight?"

Barney shook his head, hurriedly. "After last night I'll have to make an appearance at our hospitality suite and do some apologizing. Pace is probably furious."

"I'd like to take you to dinner," Charlie insisted. "Someplace nice, like Luchow's."

Barney shook his head again. "I'm sorry, Charlie. I just can't tonight." Barney then got up and left, walking briskly for the doorway and not caring whether he was being considered impolite to the speaker.

Charlie watched his friend's back as Barney receded, and he was sad. And alone again.

CHAPTER 15

"Good to see you, Dr. Russom," Colonel Roffelson said ceremoniously. "Good morning, Dr. Blakemore. How was the I-Triple-E this year?"

The three men were at Gate 12AA, right off State Route 444 and the main entrance for the Air Force Logistics Command at Wright-Patterson. It was AFLC's mission to keep United States aerospace systems in a go position wherever in the world they may be located. AFLC is immense, requiring the talent and energies of some one hundred and forty thousand military and civilian personnel around the world.

Colonel Roffelson was coordinator of the symposium and immediately apologized to Barney and Charlie. "I'm sorry we had to pull you away from New York, but we couldn't get this thing scheduled for April, like we originally planned. Washington wants us to have it now, so that somebody back there can finish a report to the Joint Chiefs."

Barney smiled at the colonel. "Never mind at all, Colonel. We are highly interested in this work, both as instrument men and as research people."

"Well, we're certainly glad to have a representative from your companies." Colonel Roffelson wheeled the car through the gate and turned right on Third Street. They followed him in their rented station wagon. He pulled up outside a long two-story building, and Barney and Charlie saw the grey facade and double rows of windows. The entrance was crested with the familiar AFLC cogwheel and star.

"That's our HQ. The only place we could set this thing up. We'll be in a temporary auditorium. Hope it's not too crowded for you. Leave your car here and we'll take you right over to the VOQ so you can clean up a bit. There's a kickoff breakfast in our cafeteria here before the first session. I'll have an aide pick you up in an hour or so."

Barney and Charlie unpacked their bags in the spacious room and Barney went to the window. "Hand me the map, Charlie," he said, as he stared across a snowy field. Charlie brought it and the two read it quickly.

"See that building way over there?" Barney said, pointing and tapping on the glass. "That's it. We're lucky they put us up so close."

Across the field, Building 828, Foreign Technology Division, beckoned to Barney. Charlie squinted through the window. He saw in the distance a light grey building facing a black-topped road. Charlie took the map of the base and spread it out on the floor. The two men dropped to their knees, and Barney traced with his finger their location and that of FORTEC.

"Look at that," he said. "This is FORTEC here— these three buildings. The main one seems to be 828, on Hebble Creek Road and Skeel. This T-296 building, the smaller one, may be it, but look at this even smaller unmarked place set back further in this field. I'll bet that's it."

"Why? How can we find out?"

"It's obvious they wouldn't build a lab for these things in the main central building. So they have to be in T-296 or this unmarked square."

"We can ask the driver who takes us back to headquarters to drive us by for a look," Charlie said.

Barney rapped his knuckles on the map and stood up again. "Well, here we are, anyway. Tomorrow night we get them." Charlie said nothing. As Barney put on another shirt, he said, "Hey, listen, Charlie. If they don't have a dinner or something tonight, or maybe right after it, it might be a good idea to take a stroll around to see whether anybody stops us. We'll walk over to FORTEC and see whether we get questioned for walking around the place."

"Do you think we should?" Charlie asked apprehensively. "Maybe that would be stretching it a bit."

"Nah," Barney waved. "We're visitors, and not the only ones on the base. We're actually above suspicion on this whole goddamn thing. There are probably fifty guys at this meeting, half of them civilians, and we all have badges, even. What's wrong with a walk after dinner?"

Charlie shrugged. "I guess so." In contrast to Barney, he found himself reaching the summit—the culmination of their plot, the turning of the switch to prove the circuit, the dropping of the shockproof watch, the first tiny breath of the prayed-for child.

A freckled-faced kid who didn't sound like more than eighteen years old called them from the lobby, ready with the car to take them to breakfast. They sat in the back in silence, as the dark blue Buick cruised the roads of the base, heading for AFLC headquarters.

"Pardon me, soldier," Barney called in the car. "Can you take us past Foreign Technology? I think it's 828."

"You mean FORTEC?" the kid said. Barney realized that it was the first time he'd heard anyone else pronounce the name.

"Yes, I think that's it. Just wanted to take a looksee."

"Sure enough, sir," the airman replied. "That won't be too much out of our way. Where are you gentlemen from?"

The kid is talkative, Barney thought. He was glad.

They turned right on Road Y and cruised for a short distance before the young airman pulled the car left off Hebble Creek. "That's it, sir," he said pointing to the right. Barney and Charlie looked out and saw the buildings, seemingly made of vertically placed corrugated steel plates. A row of hyacinths was reflected in four large glass panes at the entrance, one of which was a doorway. The entrance was surrounded by a neatly kept lawn, and through one window Barney could see a reception desk, waiting-room chairs, and, suspended from the ceiling, a model of a B-52.

The car kept going, and the airman said, "I was almost assigned there, but couldn't get security clearance because I wasn't born here." Barney just then noticed the slight trace of brogue. "Besides, they say once you're attached to FORTEC, you can't transfer anywhere else unless you're a general or something." The kid laughed, and Barney smiled as he surveyed the grounds.

The car slowed down as it came to another, smaller building. "Do they work all night in there? Three shifts?" Barney asked.

"Not every place, sir," the kid said. "But they do in there." He waved at the small building they were now passing. "I think there's a big computer or something in there that keeps going all night."

The car passed the building as Charlie and Barney memorized everything in sight. Suddenly Barney saw the tiny boxlike bunker a few hundred yards from the road, behind the other buildings. It was rimmed by a fence, and he knew it was the ELSIE electronic security system.

"What about that one way back there?" Barney called to the driver.

"I don't know that either, sir," the kid said. "As a matter of fact, it's kind of a mystery on the base because nobody ever sees any lights there, and nobody ever seems to go in or out of it. It's probably just a warehouse of some kind for old computer tapes. You know, those computers are fantastic nowadays. My brother-in-law works for IBM, and that's all he can talk about."

Barney nodded silently, and Charlie smiled to himself.

"We'd better get back for breakfast, sir. Have you seen enough?"

Barney answered quietly, "Yes, son. Thanks a lot. We've seen enough."

Dressed in a dark brown business suit, Gen. Joe Quinting bought a commuter ticket at Kennedy Airport for the next commuter flight to Washington, D.C.

Then he walked into the nearest lounge to have a drink and try to mollify his uneasy mind. He noticed two stewardesses sipping Cokes in a corner, and one smiled at him. He returned the smile, but looked back at his drink and swirled the ice with his finger.

How the hell do I get myself into these messes? he thought. What a way to make a living. Maybe I should get out of it, like I told Barney.

But he caught himself unwillingly. Joe Quinting liked his job. He liked being a general. He liked being handsome in his uniform. He even liked the hefty bulk on his hip. And he liked the security of being able to order someone to bring him anything. Like all good military men, Joe Quinting was a soldier first.

He let his thoughts continue. Now I have to kill a grave robber. Christ! But what if it's only some old geezer who gets his kicks stealing gold fillings? Jesus, what if it's only some pimply-faced punk trying to impress his fraternity brothers by winning some scavenger hunt for flowers from a graveyard? What do I do, just blow his brains out? In slow motion, he saw a bullet fly from his polished gun and smash a small wedge into a brittle skull, sending fragments of bone and flesh into soft brain, each fragment snapping like crinkled film or a broken discarded toothpick.

Well, hell. I've killed guys before. God knows how many I shot down over Korea. Is that any different? Was I shooting down a plane, or was I shooting down the bastard in it?

The bastard? Why did I call him a bastard, if I've always thought I was shooting down the plane and not the man?

What if it *is* Barney? "Hello there, Barney. How are you, old pal? Oh, by the way, I'm going to kill you. I'm going to blow your brains out because you wanted to see your brother and they wouldn't let you see him when he was right in front of you. I'm going to kill you because you overturned a few shovelfuls of dirt. Yeah, pal, that's it. I'm going to kill you because you violated the security of the United States Government. And, Barney, that's who I work for."

He snapped out of it and left his half-consumed drink at the bar. He decided to call Barney at the Essex House. What the hell, he thought. We have to talk about this thing. I've known the guy all my life and there he is a prime suspect. If we can't talk about it and get some proof or something without getting pissed off at each other, then what the hell is our friendship worth?

"Hello," he said into the telephone. "Is Dr. Russom in his room, please."

"I'm sorry, sir. He checked out very early this morning."

"Checked out? Isn't the meeting still going on?"

"Yes, sir. For three more days. I can connect you with the Pace International suite, if you'd like."

"Please."

The next voice was Dave Scott's. "Pace International, Scott speaking."

"This is General Quinting, a friend of Dr. Russom's. Is he there?"

Dave blubbered. He had never spoken to a general before. "I'm sorry, sir. He checked out to go to another meeting. Something at Wright-Patterson Air Force Base, I believe."

"Oh, shit!" Quinting said. "That's right, I forgot. He told me about it."

Scott was delighted. A general swore.

Quinting hung up and looked at his watch. It was ten o'clock, straight up, and he knew it would be nine o'clock in Dayton, Ohio. He made a mental note to call Barney there tomorrow.

"Well," the Colonel said to Barney and Charlie, "that's enough of Doppler Radar for one evening. It's nine o'clock, and you guys must be pooped." Barney and Charlie agreed, and the Colonel finished his coffee as Barney stood up.

"It's a little stuffy, actually," Charlie said.

"I'll call for the car," Colonel Roffelson said.

"Ah . . . would it be okay if we just walked back?

We know the way, and the fresh air may smell good after two days in New York."

The Colonel laughed. "Sure, if you want. But it's no problem to get a car. We have several handy for the civilians at the meeting."

Barney waved him off. "No trouble at all. We don't walk enough anyway."

Outside, a jet cracked the stillness of the night, and Barney and Charlie began strolling nonchalantly down the road. The air was chilled and the sky was cloudless. A waxing moon lorded it proudly over the bright stars and glistened off metallic building fronts, rinsing the base in tones of grey. Across the street two officers with identical briefcases strode briskly along, engaged in eager conversation.

Without saying a word, the two invaders headed toward FORTEC. They walked up the steps to the lighted lobby and looked through the locked glass door. No one was working there. A small light in the waiting area illuminated a display of foreign aircraft. Over the display, as if reassuring all who looked, hung the silver model of the B-52.

They went back down the steps, glancing down the road again, and saw no one. Then they strolled farther on and saw the lighted windows of Building T-296. They successfully fought the impulse to look in the window.

Behind the building, far off in the bare field, was the dim outline of the unmarked building which held the unknown. There were no lighted windows, no yellow outline around a doorway, no activity whatsoever.

The white limestone perimeter of the security system ringed the building with a chalk reflection. Barney stopped and stared at the small structure. In that building, he was certain, his brother had worked.

As they stood and stared, a car approached behind them and stopped. They turned as two air policemen stepped from the car and walked determinedly toward them, shining flashlights into their eyes.

"Good evening," the taller of the two AP's said in a

Southern drawl. "May I ask what you're doing here?"

Charlie was scared. Barney said, "Getting some fresh air before we turn in. We're on our way to the VOQ."

"May I see your visitors' passes, please?"

Charlie started fumbling in his pockets immediately, searching for the pink pass he had received when he entered the gate. Barney said again, "We're attending the symposium at AFLC. We just had dinner and thought we'd walk home."

"I'm sorry, sir," the AP said, "but it's a regulation that all visitors on the base within Area A must be escorted after six o'clock."

"We didn't know that," Barney said, handing the AP his visitor's pass. Charlie had finally found his own. "We just asked Colonel Roffelson if we could walk back."

The AP examined the passes under the flashlight beam as his partner looked on a few paces away, jangling a group of keys. "Mr. Russom, Mr. Blakemore, may we drive you to your quarters?"

Barney and Charlie accepted the ride, not wanting to arouse suspicion. Back in their room at the VOQ, Charlie plopped himself across the bed and exhaled deeply. "I was scared to death, Barney. I'm afraid I'm getting more than a little nervous about this episode."

"Now don't chicken out on me, Charlie. Those guys were just doing their job, and we apparently weren't supposed to walk around."

"But Barney," Charlie said, "how are we going to get to the building tomorrow night?"

"I'm not sure yet, but it shouldn't be all that hard if we walked all the way over there on the street tonight before being asked who we were."

"Well," Charlie said, "you'd better figure out something a little more definite than that."

Barney ignored the statement and slapped his hand on the armrest of the chair. "Charlie, that building is it! I know it."

"I know it too," Charlie said. "I recognized the ELSIE system."

Barney got up then and looked out the window. "And, Barney," Charlie went on, "I think I could even hear it hum."

CHAPTER 16

When Joe Quinting arrived at his desk the next morning, he placed a call to Barney at Wright-Patterson.

"Barney," Joe said without any formality, "when you finish with that crap, why don't you fly out here and spend the weekend? Maggie won't take a refusal this time, and she's a mean little bitch when good friends ignore her."

Barney, nervous now and uneasy with his friend, stammered into the mouthpiece. "I'd like to, Joe, but I can't."

"Why not?" Quinting shouted.

"Well, I'd——" Barney faltered and groped for an excuse. "Because Nancy is expecting me tomorrow, and we're going to the cabin for a week. I'm bushed after this week of seminars, anyway, and besides, I need the rest."

"Well, rest at our place. Christ, we'll leave you alone. We'll shove lasagna under the bedroom door. Tell her you'll be a few days longer. Please, buddy."

"No, Joe. . . . I——"

"You're not still PO'd about that grave business, are you?"

"No, no," Barney pleaded. "I'm just tired."

"What's the matter? You sound funny. You sound like I'm some sort of stranger. Is something bugging you?"

Barney tensed, a curt tone creeping into his voice. "Okay, Joe, I'd really like to, but I can't talk to you any more now. I'll call Nancy and take a flight down tomorrow. I'll call you."

"Don't sound so goddamn condescending. I just

thought we ought to talk some more about the other thing. Give me a call at home tonight when you finish."

Barney agreed and hung up. He would not call Joe back. He would not call Nancy. Tonight—he would wait the long hours until tonight.

The day passed slowly for Barney and Charlie. Both were restless, and both tumbled the plan over and over in their minds. Every detail had now been worked out. Charlie was confident that they could gain access to the dark buildings.

That night it was all they could do to excuse themselves properly and thank Colonel Roffelson for his kindness and the "informative seminar." They would now begin. They said they would return to the VOQ for their ostensible good night's sleep before their scheduled return to California in the morning.

They started the motor of the dark blue Chevrolet station wagon. In the back, locked securely, were Barney's black satchel and the radiating mesh belts. Under the bed of the wagon rested their special clothing, which Barney reached back for and dug out.

The first chancey step of the FORTEC conspiracy was now under way. They drove quietly, and within the fifteen mile per hour speed limit, to a secluded spot by a viaduct under Barksdale Road, across the field behind the unmarked building where they thought the creatures lay.

Working only by moonlight filtering through the windows of the car, they changed clothes. They wore dark Pendleton shirts and plain slacks, which they secured around their waists with small lengths of rope. On their feet they placed tight loafers with crepe soles. They emptied their overcoats of all pocket money and metallic objects. They drew tight kid gloves onto their trembling hands.

Dressed now for the second risk in the penetration of the small lab, Charlie drew out his special belts, and they secured them tightly around their waists. He hurriedly whispered to Barney and guided his friend's fingers along a small control box on the belt, showing him once again how to activate it, and admonished him to take tedious care to turn the radiator on at Charlie's exact signal.

For the past two weeks Charlie had carefully tested the equipment, calculating the precise mass of their bodies thus dressed. They had even procured dental x-rays to measure the metal content of their teeth. Charlie had insisted on a minimum of metal, so the tools which Barney was now extracting from his small case had been assiduously fashioned by him, in his own garage, from a nonferrous material.

They were ready.

Quietly they closed the door of the station wagon and looked across the empty field, noting the shrubbery behind which they would try to creep.

"All right," Barney whispered in a tense wheeze, "let's go." They darted into the blackness of a group of bushes and wove their way in the direction of the small building.

A plane flew overhead and a truck rolled along Skeel Avenue. The two men were black hulks as they stepped their way over the dirt and patches of old snow. Closer and closer they crept, until Barney, in the lead, could see the white outline of the lime base, shining like a saxicoline snake. He stopped, turning to Charlie.

"How close do we get?" he whispered. Charlie crept near him. "Let me go first so I can see," Charlie said, almost pleadingly. "My glasses are fogging from my breath."

Barney stepped to one side and let Charlie pass him, but kept a firm hand on Charlie's coat at they stepped even closer to the stark and quiet barrier.

Charlie stopped again when they were forty feet from the fence. "I'll go first," he said. "If it doesn't work, we can run for the car." Barney nodded and followed at a slow pace until Charlie motioned him to stop, just short of the fence. From where they stood, both men could hear the hum of power from the magnetic field.

"Don't forget," Charlie whispered. "Watch for my signal when you turn on your belt."

Barney was impatient. "Okay, okay. Go ahead." His breathing deepened as Charlie neared the low-slung web of pipe-like rods that formed the visible portion of the fence. The magnetic currents they sent out were just as tangible and it seemed to Barney that Charlie hesitated for a brief moment of involuntary tribute to this security fence. Just as well, Barney thought. Shaky movements here might spoil everything.

Now, Charlie appeared to be near the main power source. Barney watched him line himself up with some reference point, then step tentatively over a pipe that paralleled the ground at a height of about three feet.

Charlie's hands went to his belt. Barney saw a decisive movement—the flicking on of the belt switch—and then Charlie completed his step over the pipe. He stood frozen for a moment, then moved tentatively ahead for about six feet. His steps became progressively longer, climaxed by a short hop and a boyish burst of enthusiasm in which he waved vigorously at Barney.

Charley was in. He'd made it through the fence, and the power devices he and Barney wore about their belts were effective.

Barney was thrilled, and the excitement of this single brief success was taking hold of him. Now he too moved forward. He watched Charlie peering at him, visualizing his squinting eyes and knowing the strain the man's eyesight was taking throughout this entire scheme.

He could hear the fence humming, and as Charlie waved a "now" gesture, Barney held his breath and clicked on his own power switch. He felt the belt dance in vibration around his waist, as he moved forward without breathing. He shoved the small valise forward through the fence, and squirmed through himself. He fought the inclination to dart speedily to where Charlie stood, but knew the slow gradual movement would be the best. In a minute, he was standing near Charlie and clicked off the belt.

His thoughts were wild as he pushed Charlie toward the wall. They nestled there for several long moments, each breathing heavily. Barney could feel the wall of the building, a thick concrete block, probably a foot thick. He pressed his ear to the cold stone and heard nothing.

Then another truck roared down Hebble Creek Road, and the two men dashed back around the corner to the rear of the building again. When the truck had gone, Barney blurted, "Hurry up! Let's get in there!"

At the front of the building, darkened additionally by the position of the moon behind a cloud now, Barney saw the bank of liquid helium tanks which supplied the temperature control for the inside of the lab. He saw the frosted pipes leading into the wall and the pumps that regulated the flow.

Then they crept around to the entrance, next to which they saw the tall power console cabinet, resembling an upright coffin in its black rectangular outline. They pried the metal door open and inside, illuminated by Barney's small penlight, they saw the bank of frequency dividers and digital clocks, whose orange flickering numerals ticked off the seconds and hours. They crept toward the next sixty-second time window during which the inhabitant of the bunker could come or go. At that time, the security system power, as Charlie had explained, would shut itself off briefly, and the digital clock would unlock the door to the lab.

Now Charlie set to work in the darkness to remove a set of decade counters from the digital clocks, which in turn increased their gate times. This made the clocks accelerate and speed up their counting rate. The two men watched the tiny orange numerals become a blur as the first decade counter was removed.

Suddenly it was Monday morning at nine o'clock— time for Barney Russom's twin brother to enter his prison once again. "Quick," Charlie whispered. "Get over to the door and open it when it unlocks. Then I'll shut the thing down completely."

Barney stepped briskly to the small doorway and heard the dull click as soon as he arrived. He motioned back to Charlie, who then threw the master power switch. ELSIE was dead, rendered useless and incapable by the man who had designed her. And the door to the lab was now open.

They stepped inside.

With the penlights they could see they were in a small anteroom, apparently some sort of semi-office. There was a desk, on which rested several folders and books, and a chair near the far wall. On the other side was a shelf and a coat rack, a photograph of the President and an American flag. Beneath the doorway before them, they saw a thin bar of lavender light, pulsating and varying in intensity, like a faulty fluorescent tube.

They stood there waiting for their eyes to adjust. They said nothing, but both thought of what they would find. Barney envisioned a grotesque little monster, and Charlie thought again of the pathology report Barney had showed him.

Then they walked slowly toward the door, eying the thin glow beneath it. Barney shined the light onto the doorknob, and his hand almost startled him as it entered the beam of light to grasp the brass ball. He turned it very slowly.

He pushed the door quietly forward and stepped into a dim bath of lavender light, emanating from the laboratory at the end of a short hallway. Somewhere in the darkness a small motor clicked on, and some anonymous electronic monitoring equipment hummed in the glow. Barney could see a steel chair at the entrance to the lab. A white tunic was draped over it.

He walked directly into the lab, nearly hypnotized by the glowing tubes he saw banked along one wall.

There they were.

Three of the tubes were lying horizontally on a neat table spread with glassware and microscopes. They didn't glow. Electrical wires, with three plugs at the ends, dangled to the floor. The other three tubes, cylindrical, hung on the wall like fire extinguishers or circular lavender caskets. They were about four feet high, and not more than a foot and a half in diameter. They pulsed with light, and now and then the fluid within them bubbled like the tiny spires of aerating flow in a fish tank.

Barney walked toward them and shivered as he saw their contents.

The creatures had hydrocephalic heads, diminishing in size toward the chin. There was no hair, but a sort of downy substance was plastered to their craniums by the fluid within the tube. Their eyes were obloid and wrapped around the side of their heads, giving them a froglike appearance. There were two round orifices in the exact center of their faces, under which a thin slit of mouth flapped eerily in the fluid's current. They were naked, and their bodies had a greyish-white sheen, like buffed metal. There were fingers and toes, and elbows and knees, much like those of a small boy, and under their arms hung a thin fold of webbing. Barney could see beneath their skin the thin blue neon network of veins and the dark outline of a bone structure.

He was awestruck; as much as he had thought and imagined in the prior weeks, his senses were now dulled by the sheer incredibility of the nightmarish sight. Charlie brushed by Barney and peered closely into one of the tubes, and the lavender light shone through his glasses in prismatic violet pinpoints. He looked at them clinically.

"Anthropoid," he whispered excitedly. "Of course, anthropoid!"

"What? What?" Barney said.

Charlie caressed the tube lightly. "The epidermal structure. It looks like these creatures have no pores."

Barney pushed Charlie's hand off the tube. "Forget about that now," he said irritatedly. "We can look at them later. Let's get out of here!"

Barney reached up to the plug on the wall. "I'll get one of them down. You look around for anything else."

"The files!" Charlie almost shouted. "I'll find their notes and files." He swept off toward the darkness in the far corner.

Barney reached in and removed his specially made

crescent wrench from his satchel and attacked the circular brackets holding the tubes. Charlie, meanwhile, rustled papers. He came up to Barney saying, "I found a whole drawer of slides. They've taken microphotographs of the tissue. These things are what the silicon radicals were all about. Their tissue is silicon!"

"Forget about that," Barney breathed angrily, "and help me lift this tube off." The two men reached up and grunted as they unlatched the tube. It seemed to weigh about seventy-five pounds. They set it down carefully and looked for something in which to wrap it.

Barney crossed the room and saw another doorway. He motioned to Charlie and the two went in to find a cot and kitchenette, where the new pathologist apparently lived while cooped up in the bunker all week. Barney's light picked up a blue Air Force blanket, and as he reached for it, he stopped momentarily. This, he thought in anguish, was where his brother had lived. This very blanket had covered him and kept him warm.

He snatched up the blanket as Charlie tugged at his sleeve. "Barney," he said pointing to still a third doorway. "What do you think is in there?"

Barney tucked the blanket under his arm and started toward it. "Let's have a look," he said, and opened the door.

It was a small lab, almost an exact duplicate of the larger one. The tables were scattered with the same equipment and the same scopes and instruments. But this one contained a single, larger tube, hanging on the wall. Approaching it, they both shone their penlights into it.

Barney felt his stomach tighten as if suddenly squeezed by a cold and wet invisible hand. It was as if he were gazing into a warped fun-house mirror which reflected himself a hundred years hence. He felt his throat gag with a guttural cry. Charlie never heard, nor did he even notice when Barney turned to vomit.

In that larger tube, facing outward like a deformed piece of statuary, was the shriveled ochre prune that had once been Captain Robert Russom.

CHAPTER 17

The spacious apartment in Arlington was comfortable and allowed Joe Quinting to entertain frequently.

The bedroom was quiet and dark in the March chill and Potomac-iced wind. It was three-seventeen in the morning, and Quinting, who had drunk too much at a cocktail party the night before, was in no mood for love. He felt the warmth of Maggie's body next to him and her imploring caresses. Dear Maggie, he thought, I'm too damn drunk. Maggie, with whispered invitations, would not leave him alone.

The next thing he knew Maggie was shoving at his shoulder and telling him to get up.

"There's someone on the phone for you."

Joe moaned. "Who the hell is it in the middle of the night?"

"It's four-thirty, and he said it's a Colonel Rubin."

The name nudged him further from sleep, and his head still pained him. "Rubin! What does *he* want?"

Quinting rolled out of bed and, naked, shuffled to the phone.

"Yeah," he said, his voice gravelly and husky.

At the other end, Rubin was excited. "General, something terrible has happened. You have to come here right away."

Quinting moaned again. "Rubin," he said, "nothing terrible happens at four o'clock in the morning except telephone calls."

"I can't tell you about it on the phone, General. But, please. You must get here immediately."

"Well, what the *hell* is it, Rubin? Have you got a goddamned scrambler?"

"I'm not in my office," Rubin said, his voice trembling. "I'm over at FORTEC."

"*FORTEC?*" Bang. Quinting was awake. "What's going on, for Christ's sake?"

"General, we don't know how it happened. All the men——"

"Quit blubbering, Rubin. Tell me what the hell is going on, I said!"

"The phone, General. I can't——"

"Screw the phone. Out with it." Quinting's anger was mounting.

"Joe!" Maggie called.

"Well, General," Rubin went on, sniffling unsurely. "Our *Case 99* security ring has been broken." Rubin paused, and Quinting could hear him holding his breath.

Quinting was incredulous. "That's impossible, Rubin. We both know that."

"I'm afraid it's happened, General. We're all excited here. It was only discovered five minutes ago."

Quinting gripped the phone tightly and was racing to his closet as he rattled the words to Rubin. "Throw a complete security cordon around the entire base, Colonel. Ground all aircraft and scramble a squadron of 104's immediately. Call SAC and use the code name Ashtray and get me the figures on what they have up. I'll come over in an F-5 and I want you in constant contact with me on Channel W, orange frequency.

"And Rubin," he said coldly.

"Yes?" the frightened Colonel replied.

"I'll have every goddamn piece of brass on your uniform if this is as serious as it sounds." He slammed the phone down and threw it on the bed.

"Maggie!" he yelled.

It was all Barney could do to stay under the speed limit. They had made arrangements with a small private airport outside Athens, where a young charter pilot would have a plane to take them to Lake Tahoe.

The trip took four hours, most of which was taken up by animated conversation between the two excited scientists. In the back of the station wagon, rolled in the dark blue blanket and tied securely with the rope they had used for belts, the alien body turned soporifically in its fluid-filled tube. Charlie kept glancing back at it and, as it rattled against a door, he could hear the liquid swirl within it.

"I just thought of something," Barney said suddenly. "We can't open it up."

Charlie's eyes grew large. "What do you mean, we can't open it? That's why we stole it."

"That's why *you* stole it," Barney said. "I just want to make the announcement, and now it's more important than ever."

"Why? I've already set up a lab at the lake."

"It's contaminated," Barney said evenly. "That's what killed Bob."

Charlie didn't understand. "How do you know it was because of the creatures that he was like that?"

Barney choked and stared straight ahead as he drove. He again felt the queasy feeling. "Did you see his hands? They were like pig's knuckles."

Charlie grimaced at the memory.

Barney shook off the image before him. He had thought hard about Ginger's comment on Bob's hands. He compared this statement with the new rash on his niece's little fingers, and his mind refused to consider the awesome but unavoidable conclusion.

"In any event," he said to Charlie, "we can't open it. You'll have to forego your analysis."

"Forego it?" Charlie blurted. "Why?"

"Don't you realize that that's why those things were kept in that place? That that's why the place was sealed like a tomb, and only one person could enter and leave it? That that's why such an elaborate security system was wrapped around it? That that's what contaminated my brother and may already have contaminated others? You just can't open it, Charlie, until we get this thing in the open and force them to take the proper precautions against this infection."

"But there are still ways to take spectrographic examinations without actually opening the tube. We'll just be more careful, that's all. That's the reason I went along with you, Barney. Now you're reneging on me."

Barney started to wave Charlie off when he saw the airport up ahead. It was four o'clock in Ohio.

He wheeled the station wagon up to a small quonset hut at the end of a short runway. PARK'S CHARTER PORT, a small sign said above the doorway. A yellow light shone inside the office, and a dark figure waved to them from a red-striped twin Beechcraft nearby.

"You the fella that wants to go to Tahoe?" the young pilot said, as they got out of the car. Charlie went to the rear to withdraw the blanketed parcel.

"Yeah," Barney said. "All set to go?"

"We can't," the pilot said, motioning them inside. Charlie struggled with the tube, but left it in the car until Barney could lift it himself.

In the office the pilot sat down and sighed. "I hope you fellas didn't go to too much trouble to get here in time," he said. "Because we can't take off just yet."

Charlie and Barney looked at each other blankly. "Why not?" Barney asked, controlling his momentary irritation.

The pilot got up and gestured to a weather map and a teletyped message tacked to it. "Tahoe's socked in with a heavy snowstorm. Wouldn't risk going in there unless I was sure it would be cleared up in a couple of hours. Tough place to get into, anyway."

Barney interrupted him. "What about Reno?"

The pilot shrugged and shuffled some papers. "I haven't checked the forecast at Reno. Besides, I still couldn't get off the ground, even if it were clear. I just got a teletype. There's some sort of military exercise going on, I guess, and they've grounded all aircraft within two hundred miles of Wright-Pat. We'll have to wait until it's over. These things happen periodically. Usually just a couple hours' wait, unless you're a commercial airline."

Barney's eyes grilled into the pilot. "Young man, we've got to get to Lake Tahoe as soon as possible. It's absolutely imperative at any cost."

The pilot said, "I'm sorry, sir. I just can't take a chance on losing my license for the price of one charter. Even though we're just barely in the restricted perimeter."

Barney kept looking at him, thinking quickly. "Is there any way you *could* take off without being arrested or discovered, or whatever happens in a case like this?"

The young pilot shrugged again. "Well, I suppose I could. They don't really have much of a way to check all the small aircraft in the area, especially those that aren't tower-controlled, like this one. But I'd hate to take the chance. I've only been in business for a year, you know."

"Look there," Barney said, handing the lad a business card. "My name is Dr. Russom of Pace International in Palo Alto, California."

The pilot looked at the card and was visibly impressed. "Gee, you guys make some terrific equipment out there."

"Exactly what I had in mind, son. Listen, what we have in back of that station wagon is a highly complex scientific development, and it is absolutely urgent that we get it to Lake Tahoe as soon as possible."

The pilot nodded.

"If you'll take us there right away, I'll not only double the price of your charter, but if you'll send me a list of whatever instruments we make that you might need for your business here, I'll personally have them sent to you free of charge."

"Free?" The pilot was enthused.

"Absolutely free. Can you do it?"

The young man glanced at Charlie and back at Barney's card. He got up and walked to a map. "I could get you there all right. I've got auxiliary tanks on the plane, so we'd only have to make two stops. But I'd have to file a new flight plan for Reno. I still couldn't risk Tahoe in that storm."

"What about the military exercise?"

"Well, I could fly at about five hundred feet for a while on VFR to avoid any radar detection." He looked at Barney. "That's so they don't find me violating their grounding order."

Barney nodded, trying to act impressed with the pilot's jargon.

"And if we made our first fuel stop in Missouri," the pilot went on. . . .

At six-fifteen in Dayton, the airstrip was surrounded by hustling personnel, and Colonel Rubin sat nervously in a jeep as he watched the silver speck grow larger on the horizon. VHB runway was empty, and overhead the drone of aircraft was conspicuously absent. The speck gradually took the silhouette, in the reddening sky, of an F-5 jet, and its descending whine grew louder as the two puffs of burning rubber smoke signaled touchdown. Rubin winced.

The smoke trailed from the jet tires as the brakes of the aircraft were applied and the drag chute popped in a white umbrella behind it. The whine diminished as the plane turned on Taxiway 15 toward the Bass Lake area where Rubin waited. The plane stopped as technicians rushed for it. Rubin's aide started the motor of the jeep and began moving behind the men. As they drove, Rubin noticed the canopy of the plane slide back quickly and its pilot leap to the ground before the ladder was in place.

Rubin winced again.

The next thing Rubin knew, an unlit panatella was dashed at his feet. He looked into the rock-angry face of General Joe Quinting.

"Let's get over there. Get in back of the jeep, Rubin," Quinting ordered.

They sped toward FORTEC in icy silence. The sun was two vermilion orbs, reflected in Quinting's dark flight glasses. He pulled another cigar from his flight suit and jabbed it into his mouth. In the back of the jeep, Rubin eyed the woven silver-threaded stars slimmering from Quinting's shoulder.

FORTEC was rimmed with AP trucks, and white-domed and black-holstered Air Policemen were everywhere. Quinting leapt from the jeep before it stopped and Rubin hustled behind him.

As Quinting strode to the laboratory in the field behind T-296, someone snapped a short line of airmen to attention and they saluted smartly. Quinting did not return the salute. He walked directly to the fence. Rubin followed. Quinting stopped abruptly and turned to the Colonel.

"We turned it back on as soon as we discovered it," Rubin said, in what was almost an apology.

"What do you mean *back on?*"

"Someone had gotten through the fence and reset the time window and, to avoid it alarming when the window closed, disabled the system."

"How the hell did they get through that fence, Rubin?" Quinting took his cigar and tossed it into the electronic barrier. A whooping klaxon blared simultaneously with a clanking bell on T-296. The clamor of the alarms startled everyone.

Quinting turned coldly to Rubin. "Jesus Christ," he said. "Is everyone around here *deaf?*"

As they walked into the small bunker, Quinting's trained eyes noted the door ajar on the time window console beside the entrance. He walked into the vestibule and down the hallway into the lab.

He went briskly to the chair where Major Worthington sat wrapping his fingers in gauze. "Get up, Major," Quinting said to Worthington, and sat down in the chair. Worthington took a place near Rubin and frowned.

Quinting grabbed the telephone. "What's the name of the communications C.O.?" he shouted at Rubin.

"Major Reichling," Rubin said.

"This is General Quinting. Get me a Major Reichling." As he waited, he looked up at the tubes over the bench and saw one bracket empty. He glanced at the creatures in the other two tubes, then over at the unlit horizontal tubes beside him. He looked around at Worthington.

"Ugly little bastards, aren't they?" he said. Worthington reacted.

"Yes," Quinting said into the phone. "Reichling, this is General Quinting. I'm over at FORTEC. Listen, I'm expecting a message from code Camelot. See that I get it immediately. I'll be in Colonel Rubin's office for the rest of the day." Then he hung up without waiting for confirmation.

He swung around in the chair and looked at Rubin. "Did you get me that list of recent visitors?"

Rubin turned to Major Worthington. "Major, ask Corporal Westerfield outside for the list I sent for," he said, exercising his diminishing authority. Quinting glared at Rubin, not liking the delay.

He knew what name he'd find on the list, but he needed to see it in print to assuage his mounting anxiety. Soon Worthington returned and Rubin rushed to him, taking the paper from his hand and swinging it out to Quinting.

Quinting scanned the list quickly, and his eyes stopped at the name Russom, Bernard M., Pace International. Arrive: 22 Mar, 0728; Leave: 23 Mar, 2345.

"This man Russom," Quinting said. "Was he with anyone?"

"I don't know," Rubin said. "Colonel Roffelson handled the visitors to the conference that group attended."

"Well goddamn it, Rubin, find out! Don't tell me you don't know anything when I ask you. Get the goddamn answer!" Rubin shot out the doorway.

Quinting sat back, again irritated at a second delay, and took a match from his breast pocket. "Okay to smoke in here?" he asked Worthington.

"Yes, sir," Worthington said.

Quinting looked up at him and forced a smile. "I'm sorry I barked at you before, Major. Little panic, you know." Worthington nodded, smiling back. "What are you finding out about these things anyway?" Quinting asked.

"Well, sir," Worthington started, "we've got them quarantined and we're still studying their cell structure." Worthington scratched at his bandaged fingers.

"I think we'll have some conclusions before too long. They're remarkably similar to humans."

"They're not similar to me," Quinting said. "What's the matter with your hand? Burn it?"

Worthington looked at his fingers. "No, sir. Just a rash I've picked up."

Just then Rubin returned, and Quinting stood up. Rubin was pale and for the first time visibly frightened.

"What's the matter with you?" Quinting asked.

"Russom was with a man named Blakemore," Rubin said, and looked at Quinting as if expecting a reply.

"Well, for God's sakes, so what? Who the hell is Blakemore?"

The words tumbled from Rubin's lips. "Dr. Charles Blakemore of Sylmar Electronics." He paused again, and Quinting glowered at him. "He's the man," Rubin stammered, "who designed the electronic security system."

Quinting drew in a deep breath and sighed heavily. He turned to Major Worthington and shook his head in disbelief. Back to Rubin, he took a step toward the Colonel and said, "Rubin, in all my years in this business I have never seen such a blatantly sloppy breach of security. Right now I think you should know that as soon as this is cleared up, I will bring summary court-martial proceedings against you. I strongly suggest you contact the Adjutant's office immediately and prepare someone for your defense."

Rubin looked at the floor as Quinting started to leave. But the General caught a glimpse of another door and said, pointing to it, "Major, what's in that room?"

Before Worthington could reply, Quinting spun and walked toward it. He threw open the door and stood looking at the withered and shrunken form in the seventh tube. His eyes grew cold and, as he sniffed the sour odor of vomit, filmed over; he lowered them, almost reverently.

"Jesus Christ, Barney," he murmured to himself, "if they'd only told you the truth."

CHAPTER 18

The twin-engined Beechcraft glided smoothly into the blue Missouri sky over Jefferson City and set its way once again toward the West. The young pilot resumed his chatter at Barney and Charlie, talking about flying and other inconsequentials, as far as Barney was concerned. It wasn't long before the days behind them started to work their toll, and Charlie drifted off to sleep in the rear seat next to the upright tube wedged between the seats in the luggage compartment. Soon he began to snore.

Barney, too, was sleepy. Nervous and edgy, he had tried to keep up a conversation with the pilot, but his mind was racing ahead to Tahoe.

The young man asked, "What kinds of stuff do you work on, out there?"

"Mostly research," Barney said drowsily. "But I do too much traveling to get into design work."

"Do you make a lot of airplane stuff?"

"No," Barney said, as he stifled another yawn. "Mostly smaller gear, but you could probably use some of it. Transmitters and things."

The pilot thumbed toward the back seat. "What kind of new thing is that?"

Barney searched quickly for a reply. "Oh," he said, "a new kind of klystron. We have to test it as soon as we can so the Air Force can use it."

"If they're in such a hurry," the kid said, "how come they didn't fly you themselves? Charter's slower than most flights, you know."

Barney gasped. Did the kid suspect something? "Oh," he said, "they probably knew about that exercise they were having when we left."

The pilot squinted. I wonder if these guys are on the level, he thought. They made these arrangements almost three weeks ago. How come they didn't go commercial?

"Why you going to test it at Tahoe?" he then said idly.

"Look," Barney said, yawning again, "I'm getting awfully sleepy. I'd like to get some rest, if it's okay with you."

Barney nodded and stretched out as far as he could. He rested his head back on the seat and was asleep in minutes. The plane droned on, winging its way over farmlands and wheatfields, and the pilot whistled a tune to himself as he wondered again about the package behind him.

The next fuel stop was in Salt Lake City. During the leg, while the two passengers slept, the pilot had decided he would sneak a look at the so-called klystron in the blue blanket.

As they touched down, the pilot said, "There's a handy cafeteria here if you fellas would like to jump in and get some box lunches or something."

"Good idea," Charlie said sleepily, as he sat upright again. "How about you, Barney?"

Barney remembered the last time he'd eaten, and the idea shook the vision of Tahoe temporarily from his mind. "Yeah," he said, "didn't realize how hungry I was."

The plane taxied to a small area near the end of the field, and the pilot switched off the engines. Barney and Charlie walked to the cafeteria. "I don't know about that kid, Charlie," Barney said, as they waited for the sandwiches. "He was asking some funny questions when you were asleep."

"Like what?"

"Like what we had in the blanket. I think he may suspect we aren't all that official on this trip."

Charlie went to the window and peered out. The pilot was still in the cabin, but now jumped out as the fuel truck approached. "Looks okay to me," Charlie said, as he turned back to the counter.

The young pilot had watched them enter the cafeteria, and when they were gone he quickly turned in the seat and grappled at the blanket covering the tube. He stretched it open, sliding the ropes on the ends down to the tip of the tube, and unfurled the cover. He saw with wide eyes what looked to him like the body of a small child, possibly deformed. He quickly closed the blanket and slipped the ropes down again, and in a cold sweat opened the cabin door to clear the plane for refueling.

Jeez, he said to himself as he waited. That's no electronic instrument! What are they doing with it, he thought. Is it a deformed baby or someone they kidnapped and killed? Should I report them?

Wait, he thought. I could lose my license for breaking that restriction in Athens. Hell, I could tell them these guys forced me to take them to Tahoe, if there's really anything wrong. I'd better risk it and report this before I leave. Maybe there's a reward. Yes, he decided. He'd do just that.

Barney and Charlie returned to the plane and gave the pilot his box lunch. He thanked them and pretended to be checking instruments.

"All fueled," he said. "Would you guys watch the plane? I didn't want to leave it unattended with your instrument, and I have to check the weather in Reno."

"Fine," Barney said, munching. "Thank you."

The pilot walked casually across the airstrip and into a small office beside the cafeteria. He strode past a weather map and picked up the telephone.

At six o'clock in the evening, as the twin-engined Beechcraft took off once again and headed for Reno, General Joe Quinting was flying his F-5 back to Andrews Air Force Base near Washington, D.C. He was thinking of the message from Teddyrook in Moscow.

RE ALLADIN SNAFU LEAVING IMMED FOR
WASHINGTON. AM PERSONALLY TAKING
OVER INQUIRY. NEED FULL REPORT FROM
YOU IMMED SUNDAY 25 MAR FIRST THING.
BETTER HAVE ANSWERS, JOE. LOVE AND
KISSES. TRC.

Everything was going wrong for Quinting. How did
he get into this mess in the first place? Christ, he
thought. They call me in when some goddamn guy
breaks into a grave, and now they shove me into a
mess that I couldn't control because of Rubin. Now
my own ass has had it, and I have to get to Barney
and find those goddamn ugly midgets.

Joe's thoughts were interrupted by his radio beeping
to life, and a blinking light in synchronized pulsing
with the radio signaled: "Open Orange Channel."

Quinting flicked a switch and said, "This is F-5, AF
two-niner-seven-seven. Verify open. What's up?"

A voice crackled in his headphones. "Code for Orange Channel message is two-four-nine."

"Roger," Quinting snapped. He reached over to the
voice scrambler on the instrument bank. He turned
three numeral dials. Then he pulled down a small lever
which read Lock Scrambler—Message Go.

"Roger, I'm on," he said.

"General Quinting, this is Major Reichling at
Wright-Pat. Communications commander. We have
some information for you. A kid from Athens, a charter pilot, has reported something to the FBI in Salt
Lake City. He says he was forced to fly two men from
Athens to Lake Tahoe, landing at Reno, because of
weather. He says they were carrying a tubular object
wrapped in an Air Force blanket, and he took a look-
see when they had left the plane in Salt Lake. He
thinks it's a deformed kid they've kidnapped."

"What did you tell him?" Quinting asked, fingering
his control stick.

"The FBI said they told him to proceed without
arousing suspicion to Reno, where they'd have a man
waiting. They then reported to us."

"Okay, is that all?"

"Yes, sir."

"Okay, listen," Quinting said quickly. "Send a message to whoever's handling this for the FBI and our guy on the scene and tell them to let the two passengers proceed without interruption. I now know where they're going and I'll take over when I get there."

After signing off, Quinting gripped his pantella tighter in his teeth. Jesus Christ, he thought. Those dumb bastards broke into that system and carted off a trophy that's going to rock the whole goddamn world when they tell someone. And I've got to be in Washington in the morning to get my ass chewed.

Then Quinting took the cigar out of his mouth and grabbed the stick with both hands. The jet swerved quickly around, arcing in a silver reflection, and pointed toward Reno. Quinting strained against the headrest, and the skin of his face tightened. When he was turned around, he kicked in his afterburners with a heavy-handed swipe, and he swore again as his head jerked back and the plane sprang forward in an added, powerful thrust.

CHAPTER 19

The snow had stopped and the roads had been cleared. Barney drove hazardously as he wound through the mountains toward his cabin. He felt a tinge of anxiety as they approached the Agricultural Inspection station, but the guards never checked very thoroughly and they passed through with ease. Barney picked up speed and once again swerved perilously near the edge of the road as he took the turns. The blanketed tube thumped against the side of the car again.

At eight forty-five that evening, Barney steered the car roughly over the dirt road and turned into the small parking area near the river.

"God damn it to hell!" he yelled.

"Whose car is that?" Charlie said.

"Nancy's. God damn it, she's still here!" Barney's eyes burned as he fumbled with the keys and hiked up the emergency brake. He got out swiftly and opened the rear door. Charlie scurried around beside him, and the two lifted the tube from the seat. Barney kept looking furtively into the woods, cursing again at the sight of the red car.

"What'll we do?" Charlie said.

"I'll throw them out," Barney said angrily. "Let's take it up and leave it outside until they go."

"Why are they here? Did you tell them?"

"She came up when I went to New York. But she was supposed to go back to Palo Alto after the convention. *Damn* it all," he said again.

"Suppose they won't go," Charlie asked.

"They'll go," Barney said, hefting the tube and bearing the brunt of its weight. The frail Charlie Blakemore struggled and panted with his end of the tube as they began trudging through the blackness.

"Stay on the path," Barney cautioned.

The snow crunched beneath them, and in the darkness the light shadows of snow-laden branches wavered eerily as they passed under the tall trees. Somewhere an owl hooted through the crystalline air and the puffs of windborne snow prickled at their necks.

"It's cold," Charlie said with a hush.

"Don't drop it," Barney snapped back at him.

In the cabin, Ginger was tired. She had just put the baby down.

Nancy stoked the fire again and sat in an overstuffed chair beside it. She smoothed the front of her wool slacks and adjusted her headband.

She started to say something to Ginger, but suddenly Turpin jumped up with a resounding bark, startling her.

"Turp!" she said, "cut that out."

The dog continued to bark and then began to whine near the door.

Nancy became frightened when she heard footsteps on the front porch, and Turpin began barking furiously. Ginger dashed to the fireplace, as Nancy stood up abruptly. The door pounded and the knob twisted angrily.

"Nancy!" It was Barney's voice.

Nancy, surprised at the voice, went to the door and flung it open. "Barney!" she said. "Charlie."

Barney filled the doorway and dashed into the room. Charlie held back and paused momentarily on the doorsill. He was smiling meekly, a Cheshire-cat grin, and his face revealed something of a secret, like a naughty child who had wet his pants.

Before Nancy could say anything, Barney was raging at her, storming through the room, looking with anger at a Scrabble game and cards on the table. "What the hell are you doing here?" he yelled. "You're supposed to be home!"

Nancy was shocked at his temper and tried to calm him down.

Barney began to control himself as he saw the disbelief and fear on Nancy's face.

"Something important has come up. Charlie and I must be alone, and I want you and Ginger to return to Palo Alto immediately."

"It's so late, Barney."

"Never mind that, please. I wouldn't ask you to do this if it wasn't *extremely* important."

Nancy looked from Charlie to Ginger in bewilderment and confusion. Barney began throwing their luggage on the couch. Charlie walked into the rear bedroom.

As Ginger was bringing the baby into the living room, Barney saw the bandaged little hands. Then he looked with horror at the smaller almost indistinct rashes on the hands of Nancy and Ginger. My God, he thought, they've all got it.

"Your hands. . . ," he began.

"Barney, don't worry about the baby's hands. We've seen a doctor. It turns out not to be eczema but impetigo. Apparently we have all picked it up. It's going to be all right, it can be treated quickly now."

He took Nancy by the shoulders and shook her. "Look, Nan," he said, "it's not impetigo. It's what killed Bob."

Ginger stopped with a gasp, and Nancy winced as though she had just been struck. "Barney, what are you saying? Bob took his own life. I know this has disturbed you, but you've got to pull yourself together."

Barney was insistent. "Nancy, I know what I'm talking about. You and Ginger believe what they want you to believe. It may sound horrible to you, but you've got to believe me, and you've got to do as I tell you."

Nancy and Ginger exchanged a helpless glance. "Maybe," Ginger said, "you should go back to work and load yourself with work, Barney. I know that keeping busy has been a great help to me."

"I haven't got time for this," Barney's voice became strident. "I want the three of you out of here immedi-

ately. Go to Palo Alto and lock yourself in the house.
You mustn't see anyone. Not another person, do you
understand?"

Nancy bridged the distance between them and
placed her hand on his arm. "Barney, I'm terribly concerned about you. I think we should talk this out right
now."

Barney turned his back on her, his veins pulsing on
his brow, and looked at the ceiling, his hands held up
imploringly. "Please leave," he said sternly to the exposed beams. "I want you out of here and I want you
out of here immediately. I promise you I'll have the
best help in the country in just a few days."

"What *are* you talking about, Barney! Help for
what?"

Still without turning back to her, he bent and
slammed his fists against a wooden lamp and set it
sprawling with hollow reverberations across the floor.
Turpin bellowed again and kept running back and
forth.

Charlie Blakemore peered from his room and shut
the door against the noise.

Nancy moved swiftly. With tears beginning to trace
wet latticework along her flushed cheeks, she walked
determinedly to the closet and snatched her purse from
a hook. Then she took two heavy coats from a chair
and brought one to Ginger.

"Get the baby's things, Ginger. We're leaving."

Ginger went into the other room and emerged almost immediately with a heavy pink afghan and a
large diaper bag. She struggled into the coat Nancy
held for her. Nancy, still holding back her tears, put on
her own coat and rattled the keys in her pocket.

Barney turned and watched them. A thin pinprick of
sadness traced a tiny, anguished line across his mind,
and he thought suddenly of how old Nancy looked. He
thought of how beautiful she was. And he thought of
how futile and absurd the entire scene had been.

They walked across the porch, not noticing the dark
blue roll propped against the railing. As they went
down the steps, Barney stood in the doorway and

called again, "You are to stay inside the house and see no one until I get back."

The women left reluctantly, heading for the car. Barney waited a long while until he heard the second car door slam. Then he turned off the outside light above the porch. It seemed an age before he heard the car start, almost as though Nancy and Ginger were debating the wisdom of leaving.

At length, the car pulled away and Barney dragged his package inside.

In the back bedroom, Charlie Blakemore began to perspire.

They were now alone.

Almost.

The F-5 howled along the runway at nine-thirty, and jerked erratically as its chute popped and it slowly rolled with a thin whine. Stead Air Force Base near Reno was covered with snow, and the network of runways spread a black grillwork on the area.

Quinting jumped quickly into a waiting jeep. Technicians climbed over the jet and a fuel truck rolled up. He rode to the Flight Operations office and, without changing out of his flight suit or removing the holster on his hip, demanded a helicopter.

His face was lined and his expression grim. The trip had been a tense one, at more than Mach One and at fifty thousand feet, with added strain on Quinting when he had had to order a refueling tanker to rendezvous with him over Colorado Springs. Now, with hunger gnawing at him and his fingers beginning to tremble, he climbed wearily into the chopper and told the pilot to head at top speed for Lake Tahoe, where a detachment of Air Police would meet him with a jeep.

At Tahoe, as the chopper whirled into sight, a crowd of arriving gamblers and fun-seekers had collected near a gate. The jeepful of Air Policemen stuck out like white pinheads on the grey surface below Quinting.

On the ground, the onlookers buzzed as Quinting strode to the jeep. The Air Police officer snapped to attention and saluted smartly as the white helmet gleamed against the dark sky, reflecting the multicolored lights of the small terminal building.

"Captain Kuest, sir. One-oh-seventh AP squadron, reporting as requested, sir!" Quinting saluted back and stood before the group.

"I'll brief you quickly, Captain. We're headed for a cabin site near here to arrest two men for a serious security breach at Wright-Patterson Air Force Base. Stand at ease until I check with the local authorities."

"Sir!" The Captain saluted again as Quinting turned away.

In the office the workers gaped in awe, and Quinting walked over to a man who looked like he was in charge. "I have to find the telephone number of a cabin in this area," he said evenly.

"Yes . . . yes, sir," the civilian almost automatically assumed he was back in the service, receiving a command. He thrust a telephone book across the counter to Quinting.

As he took the book and began thumbing pages, Quinting once again relished the feeling of authority. He could sense the outside crowd peering through the windows, and the office workers were all sitting and standing motionless, watching his every action.

He reached for a panatella. That would impress the bastards, he thought.

CHAPTER 20

Turpin was still whining, and he patrolled back and forth under the windows like an animal in a cage, every now and then stopping to cower and glare with a growl at the thing in the tube propped against the far wall.

Barney put down his pencil and looked again at the first paragraph of his press release:

> Gentlemen, my name is, etc., and I am Vice-President, etc., of Pace International in Palo Alto, California. I am here today to reveal to you an extremely important matter that has been kept secret from us by our own Government. . . .

He picked up the telephone and dialed a number. His actions were quick and his facial muscles twitched as he ground his teeth. His jaws were beginning to ache. Charlie was struggling with his microscope and poring over the slides and notes he had stolen.

"Riverside Hotel. Good evening," the syrupy voice said.

"Do you have a public relations man there?" Barney asked.

"No, sir, we don't."

"You don't?" Barney was surprised.

"I'll connect you with our publicity department," the girl said.

The next voice sounded patronizing as it came over the wires to Barney. "Hello, Henry here."

"Mr. Henry, my name is Dr. Bernard Russom. I'm

up at Lake Tahoe. Do you have facilities for a press conference?"

"Yes, sir. We have several large rooms."

"Could you set one up for me with local press and wire services tomorrow morning at, say, ten o'clock?" Barney was growing anxious as he spoke.

"Well, sir, tomorrow is Sunday," Henry said with a faint touch of reluctance in his voice. "If you can tell me more about this, it could be worked out, but Monday would be better."

"You see," Barney said, "I'm Vice-President of Pace International over in Palo Alto, and I have an extremely important announcement that we've decided can't wait. I can't tell you exactly what it is over the telephone, but I can assure you the reaction will receive immediate national coverage and generate immense excitement throughout the entire world."

Henry was impressed. "Yes, sir," he said more professionally. "I'll work on it and call you back. But can't you tell me *anything* I can give the press guys about the subject of the announcement?"

"I'm sorry," Barney said.

Across the room, Charlie suddenly looked up. "No!" he shouted, in as loud a voice as he had used in years. "No!" he yelled again.

"What was that?" Henry asked.

Barney waved annoyedly at Charlie and said, "No, I can't, Mr. Henry. But if you could arrange it, I'll call you first thing in the morning." He hung up the phone just as Charlie reached the small desk.

Charlie snatched the paper Barney was working on and held it at his side, hiding it from Barney. "What are you doing? I have to examine that thing before we do anything like that." His voice choked.

"We *can't* wait!" Barney exclaimed. "We have to tell them about it now. God knows they probably know by now who took the damn thing!"

Charlie replied, "They couldn't. How could they know?" He rattled the sheet of paper. "And even if they did, they'd never find us now."

"Don't be an idiot. When I break this story, you'll

have plenty of time to work on it." His voice got higher and he eyed Charlie's hand.

"No, no," Charlie said. "They'll take it away from us. They won't *let* us."

"Give me that paper," Barney said curtly.

"I won't! You can't do this until I've had some time with the thing. What are you saying, anyway?"

Barney gew angry and rose in the chair, towering over Charlie. "Give me that damn paper, Charlie!"

Charlie took the paper and stepped back a way to read it. He held the paper inches from his eyes, as he had always done to read through the cylindrical lenses. Barney lunged for him.

Barney's hand swiped at Charlie's face, tearing the paper from Charlie's thin fingers. His own fingers tore past Charlie's eyes swiftly, catching the steel frame of his glasses, and sending them ripping away from the startled man. They crashed onto the rug in the middle of the room.

Charlie swung his head from side to side and his eyes became slits above his puffed cheeks as he tried to see. The world to him now was a vision of blurred pastel, of kaleidoscopically hazy smears, as if looking through the film on a dirty drinking glass. Charlie was afraid to navigate or take a step, for fear of tripping, and he dropped to his knees. He began groping along the floor in panic.

Barney looked down at him and then at the glasses. In an instant, the switch of decision clicked in his now-warped mind, and he walked lightly to the rug. As if crazed by a pathological compulsion, he was forced into the act. He knew what he was doing, but he no longer had control of even his most basic physical functions.

Barney's crepe-soled shoe reached out and crushed the glasses, expunging Charlie Blakemore's precious eyesight. He watched expressionless as his foot retreated from the twisted mass of steel and glass, as if he had squashed a beetle.

The telephone rang.

When Barney put the receiver to his ear, Joe Quinting's words, exact and spaced, as if shouting at a lip-reading deaf man, blasted at him.

"What-in-the-God-damned-hell-are-you-doing?"

Barney wasn't surprised, but he said only, "Joe?"

The voice returned stiffly and lower, as Quinting strained with every mental muscle to keep from blaring a klaxon curse. "Yes, Barney," he hissed. "Joe, Joe Quinting, remember? Your old pal."

Barney said nothing.

"Listen, Barney," Quinting hissed again. "I'm coming to get you. I've just flown across the goddamn country to save your ass before they find you first. I'm in Tahoe and I'll be there in half an hour. I'm taking you back to Washington."

Barney urged the words from his throat. "The hell you are," he said. "I'm staying here, Joe."

"Will you listen for a minute?"

Barney was silent.

"I've arranged for them to brief you completely if you'll come back and surrender that thing willingly. You're still the only person who knows as much as you do, besides that kid."

"What kid?" Barney asked quickly, thinking in a flash of his diseased niece.

"The pilot you flew out here with."

"What about him?"

"He got a gander at the thing in the tube you stole. But don't worry, we can croak him with no sweat. You're something else again."

Barney understood, and he flushed again as his jaws tightened. "Like my brother!" he shouted. "Like those poor kids on the flight crew from Norway. Like God knows who else."

"Now wait a second, pal," Quinting said placatingly. "You have to understand what all this is about. Do you realize what would happen if this thing——"

"Do *you* realize what's happening?" Barney flared. "*You're* the one who doesn't know what these things are doing to us!"

"Barney, wait!"

"I won't wait, Joe! This thing killed my brother. It's infected my family. We've all been exposed, even my wife! Maybe even you, for God's sake!"

Quinting's brow wrinkled as he pondered what Barney was saying. His hand absentmindedly, almost automatically, fingered the holster at his side. "What do you mean?" he asked. Quinting knew what Barney meant.

"That little child's hand is the color of dead meat!"

Quinting could feel fear creeping into him. He had almost forgotten how to recognize it. "You mean your whole *family* has it?"

"You sons of bitches have let this thing out. Bob was infected and so is his wife. All of us could have whatever it is right now."

"Now, Barney, we're studying this thing and can treat it only if we all get together and you surrender that creature before it's too late. You can give it up in Washington and they'll clue you in completely on every detail. Your friend, too."

"You're not getting it, Joe, until I tell what you're up to. The tube is sealed, and I'm going to announce to the world what's going on."

"I'm going to *get* it, Barney. I'm coming up there right away. I'm giving you one last chance, and I'm dead serious. Everything's out the window now, Barney. Kids, families, and even you and me. It's all over, goddamn it! We've had it! You know what I have to do."

"I have a rifle here, Joe," Barney said.

"I don't care if you have a goddamned cannon. I'm coming up and I'm not coming alone."

"Stay away, Joe."

"Sorry, pal."

Just then Turpin howled loudly, and Barney looked around. He saw a patch of snow outside the window take on a strange, shadowy glow. He shuddered involuntarily as he watched the shadow turn crimson.

"Don't do it, Joe. *Please!* Let me do it my own way. They haven't even told you everything about this thing."

"Barney. Pal," Quinting pleaded. "Which of the two of us would know the most about this thing?"

"Just don't come. I'll meet you tomorrow."

"Tonight, pal."

Barney hung up abruptly. The crimson glow outside deepened to ruby.

CHAPTER 21

Gentlemen, my name is, etc., and I am Vice-President, etc., of Pace International in Palo Alto, California. I am here today to reveal to you an extremely important matter that has been kept secret from us by our own Government.

I am about to reveal to you the incontrovertible evidence of a visit to our planet by beings from somewhere else in the universe. These beings apparently crashed their extraterrestrial vehicle in early September of last year. The place was somewhere in Norway, probably Spitzbergen, north of Oslo, off the coast of that country.

The crew of this alien vessel were killed. And the Norwegian Government allowed the United States Air Force to transport them to a small, highly guarded laboratory at Wright-Patterson Air Force Base near Dayton, Ohio. Here the creatures were studied in detail by my very own brother, working under the highest possible security cover. His name, for the record, was Dr. Robert W. Russom, and he was a leading histopathologist for the Air Force.

Today, gentlemen, you will be the first outsiders to see one of the bodies of these aliens. . . .

As he read, Barney feverishly imagined the reaction of the press. The entire world would know, within minutes, with absolute proof available, and the Government would be forced to take immediate steps to act on the disease which threatened them all.

Charlie Blakemore had locked himself in the small

bedroom with his laboratory equipment. He had called out a few futile, pleading cries to Barney, and hearing no response had settled onto his bed. Now he cried, "What are you doing, you madman? What's the red light for? I can see its glow."

Just as he called, Turpin went wild. Crazed, the dog growled and barked harshly, whining as if in pain, insane with fear.

Barney saw the ruby glow get brighter, and the pages of his speech took on the tint. He was sweating. He glanced outside again and saw the light change to brilliant white. The frenzied dog ran once more through the doorway to the other room and crashed through the window in a splintering shatter of twinkling fragments, glass and fur disappearing into the blinding light outside.

Barney leaped toward the door, and inside Charlie Blakemore covered his face from the light. There was a hissing sound.

It happened very fast.

Joe Quinting stood up in the jeep and steadied himself on the windshield frame. The jeep swerved away from the river and through the parking area. He could see the rented car.

They moved roughly along the slim path toward the cabin, and Quinting peered through the darkness ahead of the jeep's lights, waiting for the place to loom before them. The jeep kept going.

He leaned further over the windshield, trying to pierce the forest with his eyes. The jeep's lights bounced from snowbanks and tree trunks, reflecting the soft shine of winter in the mountains.

Suddenly there were no trees. The lights played on a dark, smoking charred area.

"Stop," Quinting said, with more than a little alarm in his voice.

"There's been a fire!" Captain Kuest shouted. "Thank God for the snow!"

"Quiet!" Quinting ordered. "Have your men stake out the perimeter of this area."

The men, with Quinting, leapt from the jeep. "Throw on your brights," Quinting called. He strode to the center of the blackened earth and could feel the heat on his shoes. He turned back to the jeep and shielded his eyes from the bright lights. An airman suddenly blocked one light, silhouetting himself as he spread his arms to define his section of the area.

Quinting turned and looked to the opposite side. In the diminished light, he saw the white helmet of another airman, his arms also outstretched. Glancing swiftly around, Quinting was chilled in the midst of the earth-radiated warmth.

The blackened area was circular.

Then, like a darting black shadow, a snarling animal rushed from the undergrowth into the center of the circle where Quinting stood. The frothing and foaming beast lunged with a guttural roar directly toward Quinting.

With a quick motion, his actions oiled by years of military training, Quinting pointed the muzzle of his gun at the maddened animal. He fired three rounds into the German shepherd's head.

He turned swiftly, his voice cracking audibly as he shouted, "Get in the jeep. Let's get back to the road and to the nearest cabin."

The jeep backed down the path and turned at the river, swerving again soon onto a wider dirt road. In a minute Quinting was knocking at the door of a small redwood cabin.

The elderly man, his wife peering over his shoulder, was surprised at Quinting's attire. "A general," he said. "Did you see it? What was it?"

"May I use your telephone?" Quinting said politely.

"Over there," the old man said. "What *was* that thing?"

"What thing?" Quinting asked, as he went to the phone.

"Over the Russom place. The whole place lit up. Margaret saw it."

Quinting spoke into the telephone. "Operator, can you get me a direct line to Washington?"

"I'm sorry, sir," the girl said, "the switchboard is lit up like Coney Island. There's been some kind of object over the area and everyone is calling in like mad. The lines are all jammed."

Quinting put down the phone.

"What was it?" the old man asked again. His wife eagerly waited for the general's reply.

Quinting strode again to the door and managed to smile benignly at the couple. Son of a goddamned bitch, he thought.

Then he said aloud, "Probably ball lightning."

CHAPTER 22

Joe Quinting stood before the Russom home in Palo Alto, his fists clenched tightly at his sides, his jaw clamped hard on a cold cigar. He felt a needed squirt of adrenalin enter his body as the two demolition men faced him with cold, impersonal expressions.

Quinting admired their detachment. He would have to remain a machine just a bit longer. Then he could allow himself the luxury of feeling.

"You've checked the house?" he asked the demolition men.

Both nodded.

"Any occupants?"

"Two adult women, one child."

"All right," Quinting said. "Destroy it. Destroy it now." He performed a very mechanical about-face and moved quickly to the car. He attempted to light his cigar, but his control over the movement of his hands was no longer there. Moments later, he found that he could not hold back the tears that welled in his eyes.

Then he saw the first blast of flames as the demolition men walked toward the car at a businesslike pace. Quinting rolled up the car windows so that he would not hear the screams.

Joe Quinting felt the thick stick in his hands and gently caressed the various buttons on fist-fitting convolutions of the hard rubber. The red button under his index finger twinkled in the sunlight as he wove through cumulus clouds.

The F-5 was a silver speck against the indigo sky as it swerved upward and hissed defiance at the purple

157

and white mountains below. Man and machine, operating as an integrated unit, the intercourse of mind and metal. The F-5 soared higher.

Quinting scratched the back of his gloved hand and thought back to the Korean War, the last time he had had full control over such an enormous power plant. These days it was point-to-point, no nonsense, no sonic booms, no time for fooling around with this marvelous matching of pride and power. With a curse, Quinting leveled the jet and pushed the throttle to the firewall. With a leap, the plane shot forward and Quinting watched the Mach meter rise, until it had passed 1 and the light buffeting told him that on the ground below a hundred people had looked up and sworn at the plane.

What the hell, he thought. I'm going to wring this baby out of everything she's got. Quinting yanked the stick back, and the jet pointed once again to the deep blue sky and it roared up. The altimeter clicked up to 35,000 . . . 40,000 . . . 50,000 . . .

Long time since you've been through a stall, Quinting, he thought. Let's try one.

The plane swept upward still, imperceptibly slowing as it strained against the earth below, which always won. Then, as Quinting smiled assuredly, the plane balked, then shook, then evened out before it began a slow, whirling spiral, miles wide in an arc, and Quinting rested comfortably against the headrest. A rainbow of light dashed quickly across the cockpit.

I'll bring it out with no sweat at twenty thousand feet, he thought. No sweat at all.

He made it and smiled, then went through screeching maneuvers, some of which went well, some of which were beyond the ability of the powerhouse underneath him. He pressed a button briefly and fired a short burst at the horizon. The familiar, almost nostalgic, smell of gunpowder filled the cabin.

Then he leveled off and reduced his power. He reached for the voice scrambler and switched it to Orange Channel. Although he had reached his decision, some unrecalled and probably long-dead instructor spoke sternly through the archives of memory, and told Joe Quinting to file a report to his superior.

He would code a message to Teddyrook.

"Two-niner-seven-seven is reporting in, Sir." The young communications officer thrust a paper at the grizzled General.

"It's about goddamn time." Teddyrook jumped up and knocked the telephone receiver from its cradle as he rounded his desk. He limped hurriedly to the message center.

Teddyrook brushed past a major and watched the light green punched paper feed rhythmically into the teletype. The teletype translated the coded message from Quinting into a sterile flow of capital letters.

RE ALADDIN SNAFU. SUSPECTS CONFIRMED AS RUSSOM AND BLAKEMORE. BOTH DEAD. CREATURE APPARENTLY DESTROYED BY LIGHTNING FLASH AT LAKE TAHOE. SUGGEST YOU SEND TEAM TO INVESTIGATE. ACTION ALSO TAKEN TO CONTROL SPREAD OF CONTAMINATION. NECESSARY ALSO TO ORDER CREMATION OF GINGER RUSSOM, NANCY RUSSOM AND INFANT. REMAINS OF PALO ALTO HOME NOW UNDER OBSERVATION BY LOCAL AUTHORITIES. SUGGEST YOU PLACE FORTEC UNDER IMMEDIATE QUARANTINE. BELIEVE I HAVE IT TOO. CAN'T TAKE CHANCE OF TRANSMITTING FURTHER. AS PERSONAL FAVOR REQUEST LANCER TO MAKE THIS WHOLE MESS PUBLIC. BE GENTLE WHEN YOU EXPLAIN TO MAGGIE BUT KEEP YOUR GODDAMN HANDS OFF HER. SEE YOU, PAL. JOE. END.

Teddyrook ripped the yellow sheet of paper from the teletype and hobbled to the bank of direct no-code voice transceivers. He punched the transmit button for Red Channel 496.

There was no acknowledgment.

"Joe, cut that shit out!" The husky General screeched into the mike. "Get on the line, damn you!"

No answer.

Quinting was over the brown and tan quiltwork of Kansas. He stolidly watched the blinking red light demanding his attention. Teddyrook's static-ridden voice grated from his headset. Quinting's gloved hand reached over and turned the receiver off. Letting go of the stick, with his other hand he ripped his helmet off and let it drop to his lap.

This was the spot, he thought. He pulled the plane up and started for fifty thousand feet.

As he did so, he tugged off his glove and looked at the red rash on the back of his hand.

They'll never stop it now, he thought. Not with the others. Worthington never stopped it. The baby must have given it to a doctor. God knows how many in Worthington's family, in Rubin's family . . . everywhere. He had done what he could to slow it down, he thought.

He could imagine a press conference, when the Government would finally realize how silly the secrecy had been, when they would at last bring in every damned medical genius in the country to stop it—not just one pathologist in a concrete blockhouse.

He pushed the stick forward and for the last time rubbed the raw red rash on his right hand. The plane screamed earthward and the fields of Kansas filled his windshield.